I0557308

P.N.G.

Persona Non Grata

PAUL CHARUKA

Copyright © 2020
PAUL CHARUKA
P.N.G.
Persona Non Grata
All rights reserved.

No part of this publication may be reproduced, distributed, or
transmitted in any form or by any means, including photocopying,
recording, or other electronic or mechanical methods, without the
prior written permission of the publisher, except in the case of brief
quotations embodied in critical reviews and certain other non-
commercial uses permitted by copyright law.

PAUL CHARUKA

Printed in the United States of America
First Printing 2020
First Edition 2020

ISBN: 978-0-578-72664-9

10 9 8 7 6 5 4 3 2 1

Cover art by MiblArt

Disclaimer
P.N.G. reflects the author's best recollections of events. In order to
maintain individuals' anonymity ALL names mentioned in this book
have been altered. For artistic purposes specific details, event spaces
and times have been compressed, changed or embellished.
Hence, NAMES, characters and places appearing in this book are
either the product of the author's imagination or have been altered.
Any resemblance to actual persons, alive, dead or undead, Federal
agencies, business establishments, events and locales are ALL entirely
coincidental.

P.N.G.

TABLE OF CONTENTS

Prologue...1

1 ....*3*

Cops For A Few More Hours

2 ....*22*

Training For A War Zone

3 ....*30*

Afghanistan, Graveyard Of Empires And Security Contractors

4 ....*45*

Salang Pass, The Tunnel Of Death

5 ....*62*

Knock Out Bats

6 ....*81*

Convoy Missions, Prospecting & The Dreaded Nds

7 ....*94*

Trouble

8 ....*110*

P.N.G.'D Afghanistan

9 ....*122*

Back Home, Regouping, Plotting

10 ....*136*

México

11 ....*155*

Gold Fever

12 ....*185*

Million Dollar Moment

13 ....*225*

P.N.G.'D Again But With Parting Gifts

14 ....*248*

One Last Time

About The Author..*261*

PROLOGUE

I, well, I mean we, are still alive and survived an incredible odyssey in search of riches where we faced the gravest of life threatening dangers as well as the threat of long imprisonment after running afoul of government bureaucracies.

I really can't say if we're completely in the clear because there're still too many loose ends but for now, I think it's safe enough to tell our story. Let me introduce myself, my name is Salvatore Rossi. I go by the name Sal. I'm of Italian descent, yeah, I've been known to be impulsive, with a short fuse and a get rich-quick schemer! I've been a dreamer all my life, looking for adventure and riches. Too honest to be a gangster but too dumb to be a businessman so I did the next best thing, I became a cop.

Now my police partner Daniel Mahoney, or Danny as he's called, is my complete opposite. He's an affable, gentle giant of an Irishman, slow to anger but able to slug it out with the toughest hoods in our city's mean streets.

For me and my partner Danny, our odyssey began on our last shift of our very last day before we retired as members of the Washington, D.C. police force and culminated when the winds of fate blew us across the United States – México border.

1

"There comes a time in every rightly-constructed boy's life when he has a raging desire to go somewhere and dig for hidden treasure."

Mark Twain, The Adventures of Tom Sawyer

It was 2002, a bitter, cold December 23rd, an almost Christmas Eve night when most folks of this city were warm and snug in their homes. Just a few minutes past midnight, only a couple hours left before the end of the midnight shift and the beginning of our official retirement.

On that harsh December night, my partner and I were sitting in our patrol car counting down the minutes before our shift finally ended. The windows of the patrol car were slightly rolled down allowing the bitter cold to hit us like a slap to the face. It had been our habit whenever the cruiser was parked to have the windows down slightly so that we could hear and see anything that might sneak up on us. Our breath was visible while we talked and we frequently warmed our hands on the vents blowing hot air.

I had been working on Danny for many months, trying to convince him to join me on a convoy security job in Afghanistan. To say that Danny was not adventurous is an understatement. I knew the question wouldn't get a warm reception but I had to know where his head was. "Hey Danny, you made a decision on that convoy gig in Afghanistan?" I inquired.

"C'mon on, Sal, we're not even one second into our retirement and you want to head off to Afghanistan. No, no way man!"

That resolved the matter as to where the big Irishman's head was at so I tactically decided to postpone the issue for a later time. "Sheeeet Danny! Can you believe it? Tonight's our last night of work! We'll be on leave for our last two weeks on the force then just stroll into headquarters on Monday, January 5th," I paused and raised my voice, "civilians again!" which merited a double high-five!

"Hey man don't change the subject, I'm not getting involved in another one of your cockamamie schemes! Remember the time we went scuba diving with metal detectors looking for gold from a sunken Spanish Galleon in the Florida Keys?"

"Yeah, I remember but we didn't have enough time to really search...I"

Danny abruptly interrupted me, "time to search? That big ass shark came at us and I got the detector headphone cord wrapped around my neck while trying to evade that freakin gaping mouth, I nearly drowned!"

I threw my head back and laughed heartily as that mental picture formed in my head.

Danny laughed bitterly, "It's funny now but not back then! Look, all I'm interested in right now is becoming an ex-cop, have a decent pension coming in every month and no longer having the burden of trying to solve society's problems every damn day."

I shook my head in total disapproval. "Not very ambitious partner!"

"Oh wait, I forgot," he paused then resumed, "yeah, I wanna sleep! Sleep for a month!" he said in a low trancelike tone. "Maybe some mornings I'll have steak and eggs for breakfast then go back to sleep again! Yep, that's all I want!" as he sighed with a smile and a far-away look on his face.

I laughed and affirmed what he was saying, "OK, I'm with you on catching up on twenty-five years of sleep deprivation but that's short term stuff brother. If we're going to keep our long term dream alive we're going to have to dive head long into some very risky ventures!"

Danny glared at me and didn't say anything.

Changing topics quickly, "Hey man looking back doesn't it seems like our time on the force was a blink of the eyes. Just the other day we were having fun and getting into trouble in the academy." We both chuckled because in general we were of the same mindset. We became cops to fight crime, drive fast and carry a gun. So the boring classwork during the six-month academy certainly brought out the mischief in us much to the ire of the academy instructors.

Keeping the conversation light I asked, "Hey you still going to your in-laws in Florida for Christmas?"

"Yep, gotta do it for Becky. If she doesn't see her mom and dad during the holidays she gets the blues."

"Pff! You gotta love that Florida Christmas feeling, 85 degrees, and 85% humidity! No way man, not for me!"

"Who cares Sal, I leave tomorrow for Florida on my Christmas vacation, then come home, turn in my gun and badge, finish out-processing and become a civilian again! That's really something worth looking forward to!"

I couldn't argue with Danny's thinking, I too was certainly looking forward to being a civilian again. No midnight shifts, working weekends and having to deal with more assholes than toilet paper plus the freedom to work on my treasure hunting bucket list, yeah I could get used to that!

"In total agreement Danny but just hear me out. For the first time in our lives, we finally have the time and means to make really big money. That convoy security gig in Afghanistan that I've been working on pays 12K a month which is a gold mine in itself but the beauty of it is that we're going to have a lot of downtime to prospect for gold and gems on the slide. I'm telling you it's going to be like taking candy from a baby and… "

Danny hotly interjected, "How the hell did you get this information? Who would give up info on a big score like that?" he scoffed.

"Man I've got a *gray* file that's more far-out than the X files!! Listen, you know I served in the Corps back in the '70s. Well, a guy I served with, Scott, a good buddy of mine, he stayed in the Corp for twenty-five years. After the Corp, Scott got into the high risk contracting world mostly in Africa but he told me he recently spent two months in Afghanistan doing some secret squirrel shit and that he was able to locate some incredible sites with gold and gems that were easy picking."

"Well, did he get some of the gold or what?"

"The truth is yes and no."

Danny rolled his eyes in disbelief "Uh-huh! That's about right."

"It's not what you think Danny, he did recover some gold and gems but sadly Scott was killed when his SUV flipped over and rolled down a mountain in northern Tajikistan. However, before his accident, he emailed me GPS grids for two different areas which just happen to be the routes we will be traveling on our convoy missions. He said that both of those areas would on occasion yield gold nuggets the size of marbles! "

"That's fantastic but if he's right and we start tapping into the mother lode, how the hell do we get it back home?"

"C'mon man! You know I always have every angle covered! This is how it's going to play out. We'll ship our spoils home once a month so no one gets suspicious. I got a connection at a specific military post office in Kabul. I give the dude $200 cash per shipment and it arrives home without any fuss, you know what I mean? I'm telling you we're going to get paid on both ends!"

Danny replied, "Hell, we've been cops for twenty-five years, we've been shot at, stabbed, punched, spit on and nearly fired several times. Don't you think once we ought to out-process first then just let off the gas pedal for a while?"

"I get what you're saying Danny, but after we make the big score then we can relax and stay off the gas pedal forever!"

"Look, I won't lie, I could use some extra dough for my daughter's college tuition and that RV me and Becky been wanting to buy but," he paused, "but deploying to Afghanistan? It's just a no go without Becky giving the green light. Anyway, I don't want to talk about that crap right now. We've got two hours left of the shift, let's finish it without any drama, I'm getting really nervous, I just want to get out of this cruiser and call it a career! Can we do that at least?"

"Hey man don't sweat it, it's dead out here we haven't had a call in . . . "

Of course fate has no sense of humor as the gruff voice of the police dispatcher boomed our call sign out of the console speaker and as always sounding like he was gargling with a mouthful of marbles.

"Scout 20!"

"Damn, here we go, you get tired of being right all the time?" Danny said with a worried expression on his face. Danny sitting on the passenger side grabbed the microphone from the mobile radio charger. "This is Scout 20, go ahead dispatch."

"Anonymous caller to 9-1-1 line states there's a man at 3rd street and Jefferson drive possibly selling drugs, caller also said that the subject appears to have a holstered handgun in his waistband. The suspect is described as a dark male in his late 20's-early 30's, very well dressed, possibly a black suit and dark dress topcoat, respond Code 1."

Danny responded, "Scout 20, copy, in route!"

Danny turned toward me with a worried look. "Sal, that's a helluva lookout and it's within sniffing distance of the U.S. Capital portico not an area where drug deals go down plus that dude sounds like he's dressed for the opera."

I nodded in agreement, "Yeah partner, sounds not right to me."

"This shit can't be happening Sal, it's Monday, it's freezing, two days before Christmas, we're almost civilians and now we have to respond code one."

I laughed and reassured Danny, "Relax, this is a nothing call, we'll get there and you'll see it's a bogus call, everything is going to be just fine."

Danny activated the lights and siren and I punched the patrol car into a hasty departure. "Hey Sal, I'm serious, no heroics, OK? We're not arresting anyone, no five hours of paperwork and countless court appearances and for God's sake, don't fire your weapon unless it's life or death! We've got pensions in our back pockets. We don't want to wind up at the Internal Affairs office in the morning and possibly the department holding up our retirement, you hear me?"

I nodded with agreement but with a grin on my face. I knew no matter what, Danny would do the right thing in a pinch.

Danny shook his head with great apprehension as the patrol car sped off. "Holy shit, I'm never going to get my pension! I feel it, it's just too good to be true, I'll never get it!"

I continued driving while grinning ear to ear.

"Listen to me just this once Sal! If we find the dude, stay behind cover, yell at him to freeze, if he doesn't run we'll pat him down do a field observation report and send him on his way."

"And if he runs?" I countered.

"Well, if he runs away then that's the end of it! We're not chasing anyone with only hours before we retire!"

I concurred with Danny's plan, "Ok, agreed!"

Out of habit, Danny turned off the lights and siren about a mile from the suspect's possible location. As we got nearer I turned off our headlights and reduced the speed of the cruiser to a crawl. As we rolled down a long street with cars parked on both sides, we spotted the suspect.

I immediately stopped the cruiser and whispered, "Well there he is, let's go and get this over and done with!" I didn't have to say anything else to Danny, we'd use these same tactics hundreds of times before. We exited the cruiser and did a crouched combat walk on the street side of the parked cars to avoid detection. The closer we got to the suspect the less he looked like your basic street dealer criminal. The suspect was partially hidden by leaning against the recessed part of the commercial building wall. He basically boxed himself in making it difficult for him to run away, not very clever and very unusual which heightened my alertness. As we got within ten feet of the suspect, he continued to look in the opposite direction toward the intersection so he never spotted us. It was clear that the suspect was a Hispanic male, very well dressed to include shiny dress shoes, all very peculiar for a street dealer. As we continued to observe his movement, the wind blew the right edge of his coat away from his body which clearly showed a holstered handgun. We knew it was time to act. I looked at Danny and signaled him to move with a nod of my head. He knew the drill, without a word spoken, Danny moved about ten feet to my right. When he was in position, we looked at each other and I gave him a silent one, two, three count at which time we simultaneously popped up from opposite sides of a parked vehicle and gun faced the suspect. In unison, we yelled, "Police don't move! Hands up or we'll shoot!"

The suspect was definitely caught off guard, he had no idea we were there and had little chance of escape without getting drilled. The suspect drew back attempting to fade into the shadows of the building all the while scanning the area with a wild look on his face, no doubt looking for a possible avenue of escape. I immediately yelled at him,

"Don't even think of running, you'll just die tired, my 9mm is faster than you."

Danny called out to me in a loud whispered tone, "Sal, don't shoot we have cover!"

The suspect nervously held the right side of his coat where we had seen his holstered weapon. "Man, I'm not going to jail, I'm just here making a pickup to keep my family safe."

Without taking his eyes off the suspect, Danny called out to me, "What the hell is he talking about Sal?"

"Dunno, but this dude is involved in some serious shit."

As usual, when negotiations were needed, Danny took the lead. Danny called out to the suspect, "Look, we can work this out! What's your name?"

"My name? Shit! You're trying to distract, I'm getting out here one way or another!"

In a commanding voice, Danny gave the suspect the ultimatum, "Listen good, here's the deal. We know you have a gun, we can't let you keep it! You put the gun on the ground and we'll let you run away. You keep tugging at your gun or you pull it out, you die. Hurry up and decide. Last time, what's your name?"

With some trepidation, the suspect responded, "Yeah, Ok, I'm Manuel but I'm called Caballo."

Trying to close the deal on this mess Danny asked, "Caballo?"

The suspect responded, all the while scanning around nervously, "Like I'm a fast runner like a racehorse. So just like that, you're going to let me go if I put my gun down?"

"Yeah, just like that. It's Christmas you know," Danny reassured him.

"Alright, Santa Clause so your partner is not going to shoot me when I take my gun out and put it on the ground?"

"No, he won't. Look, my name is Danny and officer friendly to my left is Sal. We don't have much time before our backup arrives."

I couldn't believe Danny gave the perp our names. I turned toward Danny and countered, "Have you lost your mind? We're going to let him go and he now has our names?"

Danny responded without taking his eyes off the suspect, "What the hell difference does it make if this asshole gets to spend Christmas with his family? As long as we get the gun off the streets, we've done our job!" With the sound of sirens now getting closer Danny turned his immediate attention to Manuel, "Manuel, you can hear the other cops coming. Once they get here the deal's off! So put the gun on the ground and get the hell out of dodge!"

With the impending arrival of additional police officers, Manuel's eyes bulged with fear. He gingerly pulled his gun out of the holster and laid it on the ground, never taking his eyes off the officers.

I commanded Manuel one last time to keep his hands up and not to move after he laid the weapon on the ground. Me and Danny slowly approached the suspect, guns drawn and aimed at center mass.

In a calming voice, Danny told Manuel, "Stay cool." We got within three feet of Manual, and we stared at each other for what seemed like an eternity. Danny finally commanded Manuel, "Alright Manuel, get the hell outta here, quick shit!"

Manuel still skeptical began walking away slowly, once he was out of reach he turned toward us with a half-smile and yelled, " Merry Christmas Santa Clause!"

Danny replied, "Enjoy Christmas with your family." Manuel took off running at an incredible speed living up to his nickname of the horse.

We picked up the weapon which turned out to be a huge Desert Eagle .44 Magnum semi-auto handgun. Making the situation even more bizarre, a cursory inspection revealed that that the lower handgun receiver did not and never had a serial number. A strong indication it was a black market manufactured lower receiver, no doubt made by a professional which added to a mystery that we'd probably never unravel or so I thought. I just shook my head and told Danny, "Glad we didn't get into a shootout against this cannon!"

"Damn straight Sal."

The backup unit arrived coming to a screeching halt just a few feet from where we were standing. Two young officers in their early twenties jumped out of their cruiser. The passenger officer yelled out in an excited voice, "Where's the suspect?"

"We recovered the gun but the suspect bolted, really dark here, didn't even get a good look at him. Couldn't tell if he was white, black, Asian or Bigfoot" replied Danny.

I echoed Danny's assessment, "Yep, nothing to see here kids!"

Clearly annoyed, the driver of the patrol car groused, "Man you old-timers, it's time for you two to retire." Both officers shook their heads with disdain, got back into their cruiser and sped off with tires squealing.

"They got that right, ay Sal?"

"Definitely partner, time to retire. Let's head to the station and get this weapon checked into the property locker and call it a night!"

"The best thing you've said all night."

Our last shift finally ended, we checked out with the desk sergeant and went our separate way . As planned Danny went to Florida to enjoy the warm weather with Becky and his two daughters. I relaxed and spent quality time with Jean and my seventeen year-old son Victor who was fast becoming a man. Victor was going through the application process for the U.S. Military Academy at West Point and we were anxiously hoping for a conditional offer from the Academy.

Well, the fifteen days of leave went very fast, it was January 6th, 2003, so after twenty-five years and four days, D-day, finally arrived and not a nano second too soon as I was itching to get to police headquarters and turn my police shit in and instantly become a civilian! After wearing a uniform for six years in the Corp then twenty-five years in the PD, I was ready to never don a uniform ever again!

We had prearranged to meet at police headquarters on January 6th at 0845 hours so that we could be the first ones to out-process. I arrived at HQ at 0830 hours, a full fifteen minutes early but Danny was already there with his arms crossed looking impatient. I parked my car and walked up to Danny, "Top o' the mornin to ya me boy."

Danny smiled and said, "Hey, stop talking Irish!" as we both chuckled, shook hands and quickly headed into the building. We punched the cipher code and entered the massive police complex. We walked the long, stark corridors to the out-processing office of Captain Wazluski. We knocked on the door before entering and right away encountered Captain Wazluski. We greeted the captain who was seated behind his desk but even though we were scheduled to out-process this morning, he looked annoyed that we were interrupted his super, duper important paperwork.

"Alright, men, c'mon let's see your sign out sheets." The overweight, spectacled, desk-bound, never a warrior captain, inspected our out-processing forms and frequently mumbled affirmations signaling that all seemed to be in order.   In the meantime, me and Danny periodically glanced at each other sweating bullets hoping that   Captain   Wazluski   wouldn't   discover   any discrepancies that could delay our official retirement.

"Uniforms check, Sam Browne duty belts check, holsters, assorted gear, check, nightsticks aha, alright fellas, looks like everything is accounted for, now it's time to give up your service weapon and badge." Without saying anything to the captain we handed him our unloaded semi-auto handguns, three mags and badges. Inspecting the serial number of both weapons, the captain continued mumbling, "Aha, aha, serial numbers are correct, three mags each, active duty police IDs and badges each, perfect! Alright men, everything is accounted for, here's your retired police IDs and badges. Congratulations, you both are now officially retired and PNG from the W-D-C-PD!"

"What the hell is PNG Captain?" Danny asked thinking that it was something derogatory.

Looking jovial for the first time, the captain responded, "P.N.G., Persona Non Grata, means no longer welcomed here. You two are now civilians. Your first pension check will pop into your bank accounts the first of every month starting February 1st! Enjoy your life men! You've earned it." We shook hands with the captain and walked out of HQ as fast as possible before anyone tried to stick us with unfinished business.

As we walked to our cars in the parking lot, Danny blurted out, "Hey man, I don't think I can make that Afghanistan gig, you go without me," looking down sheepishly.

"Danny!, what the hell! I already committed us to the Rapid Action company project manager! We're scheduled to attend the four week vetting course in early March. Once we complete the course, we go home on leave for two weeks then deploy to Afghanistan and take over the convoy security job." I said with a hint of rancor.

"Man, oh man, I never gave you a firm commitment to that lunatic idea!"

"Hey, fair is fair, why don't we let the gold lady luck decide?" Lady luck was my 1907, Saint-Gaudens double eagle, gold coin that was passed on to me by my dad. He carried it in his pocket as a soldier in both the Italy campaign and the push into Germany during World War II and I carried it in my pocket during my twenty-five years on the PD.

"You asking me to decide something as insanely dangerous as this on the flip of that dumb gold coin you always carry?"

"Yea, that one! C'mon, you got a 50-50 chance, how about it? "

"Pff" he muttered accepting the challenge. "Go ahead flip it."

I flipped my highly scratched coin up in the air, end over end it went. "Call it Danny!"

"Heads," he yelled with confidence.

2

TRAINING FOR A WAR ZONE

It's been said there is something about a buried treasure story that affixes to a man's mind. He will pray and curse about the day he heard of the tale. He will let his last hours on earth come upon him still believing he missed finding the treasure by only one foot. He will never forget about the riches that eluded him even while taking his last breath in this mortal world! - Unknown

2003

Tails it was!

Although Danny isn't an adventurous person, he is a man of his word. Needless to say the coin toss wasn't the deciding factor, rather the looming expenses of sending his two daughters to a top tier university was enough for him to argue his case with Becky.

I knew it would be difficult for Becky with Danny being away from home during their daughter's last year of high school before leaving for college. However this sacrifice would end most of their worries of having to go through the painful loan application process for their daughter's college tuition then having to make monthly payments for a decade or more. I think that was certainly a strong selling point for Danny to exploit. At least that was the approach I suggested he use!

Becky was steaming when Danny once again mentioned the subject of going to Afghanistan. "You're going to blindly follow Sal over the cliff?"

"Now hon, it's not that dangerous of a job plus . ."

"You think I don't read what's going on in that hell hole of a country?"

"Just hear me out, 12K a month in salary plus any gold and gems we ship home, I mean we'll . ."

"Danny, yes we could use the money but me and the girls need you more than the money!"

This went on for a couple of hours before Becky tearfully relented.

At my house, I'd been in conversations for months with Jean prepping her for the eventuality of me leaving for the Afghan gig. Although very unhappy at the prospect of me working in such a dangerous place, we'd been together long enough to understand, as she called it, my

'Don Quixote' quest. So she didn't try to talk me out of it, just a few promises to not take any outrageous risks and to return home safely!

After a couple of months of lounging around the house I was getting restless and ready to get my post retirement activities started, however on the eve of leaving home for the mandatory four week vetting tactical course in the Carolinas none of us slept well. This course was a pass or fail mandate for us to be able to deploy on the Afghanistan convoy security contract. The following morning we all got into one car for the drive to Dulles Airport. Conversation was light with no serious talk as everyone's doubts and fears remained hidden and unspoken.

At the airport reality set in for sure, teary goodbye for the wives and a bit of separation anxiety for me and Danny since neither of us had ever been separated from the gals for more than a couple of days.

I remember Beck's last words to me, she looked me straight in the eyes and said, "Sal, you keep my man safe, you hear!"

I thought it was kind of funny since Danny was a giant who could tear a man in half like a piece of paper. I replied with a reassuring look, "you can count on it Beck!"

We said our goodbyes and assured them we'd be home in about four weeks before heading to our Afghan assignment.

We flew a circuitous route to a remote region of the Carolinas and then onto a secluded training site with thousands of acres that seemed more like a military installation. We would be billeted on the compound for the entire four weeks of training. We found our sleeping accommodations less than stellar with an open bay with our own personal cot.

The entire first day was all in-processing that consisted in equipment issue, a ton of paperwork, a medical exam along with blood work. Whether it's the military or law enforcement, there's always one guy that can't handle needles and this time was no exception. They stuck this big muscled guy with the proverbial 21 gauge needle in the vein for just a couple of vials of blood and he went down to the ground like a WWE wrestler! Yep, a bunch of us had to pick up his embarrassed ass off the floor. Of course for the next four weeks he was the butt of a lot of jokes and laughter.

We had our first meal which wasn't too bad and then finally to the bunkhouse to call it a day. All of us shot the shit for about an hour then one by one dropped out unto our cots. Funny as shit moment when Danny laid on his cot, the tall Irishman's legs stretched well past the edge of the cot. The instructors were good about things like that and always tried to accommodate us when possible. The following night they brought us gym matts that were two inches thick for tall personnel or those who preferred sleeping on the floor. From that night forward, Danny slept on the matt and was able to get some good sleep.

Our class consisted of sixteen security contractors all bound for Iraq or Afghanistan on different contracts. We got to know each other and discovered that our gig was very unique due to the fact that we'd have the freedom of running the roads unlike the other contractors who were going to be in highly regimented security projects.

The vetting course began with a fitness assessment which we were informed by the instructors is where many candidates wash out. The physical efficiency battery test entailed a 1.5 mile timed run, a timed sprint course, sit and reach test and a requirement to bench press seventy-five percent of our body weight, a breeze for all the contractors. When it was Danny's turn to do the bench press test, he ordered the instructors to load the barbell with three hundred-fifteen pounds, which he easily bench pressed ten times, everyone was impressed, I mean everyone! The weapons qualification on the M4 carbine and M203 grenade launcher, 9mm pistol, 12 .gauge pump shotgun, and two different types of machine guns was also a breeze.

Once all those prelims were done we began the two phases in the VIP protection section. First phase was the team movement drills which included bounding, contact drills, peeling and crossing danger areas which would turn out to be extremely useful in Afghanistan. The second phase consisted in walking formation drills, motorcade arrivals-departure drills, live-fire attack on principal drills along with armored vehicle skills. The reality of this part of the training, it just became boring and tedious like learning ballroom dancing. After the twentieth repetition most of us just went through the motions so as not to piss off the instructors too badly.

The final day of the vetting course finally arrived. We had our graduation ceremony, at its conclusion the lead instructor handed everyone their contract and an envelope that had their names on the outside containing airline tickets and other relevant deployment itinerary information. We signed on the dotted line on our one year contracts then opened our envelopes which left us dumbfounded! Prior to attending the vetting course we were informed by the recruiter at the Rapid Action Protection Company (R.A.P.) that we would get to return home for two weeks of rest before deploying to Afghanistan. However, our tickets told a different story, we were ticketed for a departure to Afghanistan tomorrow! The flight itinerary was for a departure from the Carolina airport to Atlanta Hartsfield-Jackson International followed by a flight to Dubai International then straight into Kabul International Airport.

Although we received a direct deposit payment of one hundred dollars per day during our training, our envelopes each contained one thousand dollars in cash. A note inside the envelope from the R.A.P. corporate office, apologized for the unexpected change in deployment date but due to the instability in the region, it was imperative for us to get down range as soon as possible. The money was for us to use as needed for the purchase of clothes, footlockers and any other incidentals we might need, no expense report required! We both grumbled at the change but thought it was very generous of the company to dish out that much dough to us.

We quickly notified our wives of the change in travel plans. They were understandably upset but realized there were no other options. Straight up truth, after only four weeks away from home we both were a bit homesick. Jean and Becky already had our forwarding address in Afghanistan so we asked them to ship our gold pans and other assorted prospecting gear to us as soon as possible.

Due to our exigent circumstances, the training site manager generously lent us one of their trucks for us to use as needed for the rest of the day.

We went into the city and bought footlockers with wheels, a few more pairs of BDU's and a shit load of power bars.

3

AFGHANISTAN, GRAVEYARD OF EMPIRES AND SECURITY CONTRACTORS

*The number of people who would be willing to leave the
comfort of their home and work as a gun for hire in
Afghanistan is small. However the number of folks willing
to work as a gun for hire and simultaneously search for
treasure in Afghanistan is infinitesimal! To find treasure
one must be fully committed and unafraid to risk it all.*
Sal Rossi

April 2003

The next morning we departed the training facility
and everything after that and up until the time we
arrived in Kabul is a blur. Maybe two days in
transit with an overnight stay at a real fancy hotel in
Dubai. The company had a credit card on file with the
hotel which authorized us to order anything we wanted
and eat as much as we could. We never left the hotel and

needless to say Danny ate as much as a group of Marines after a week in the field.

The next morning we took a cab for the Dubai Airport. The airport was confusing but we quickly figured out how to maneuver through a city sized airport and found our flight to Kabul. Eventually we arrived at the Kabul International Airport late in the morning with butterflies in our stomachs not knowing what to expect.

As we made our way out of the terminal it felt like we walked into a pizza oven, Danny grumbled, "holy shit it's hot, where do we go from here?"

"We're exactly where we need to be" I quipped. Then the strong odor of human waste hit me, "What the hell is that smell?"

Danny replied back with a cringed expression, "I don't know but I hope the whole country doesn't smell like that!"

"Hey Danny let's follow the crowd. Everyone seems to know where they're going." And that's what we did, like lost children we walked away from the terminal and followed the horde of passengers to an adjacent parking lot.

Now it was my turn to grumble, "Damn, this is hotter than Florida in August."

Danny nodded and said, "Aha!" with a smirk on his face.

After thirty minutes or so most of the passengers we followed to the parking lot had been picked up by their company vehicles and departed. Now it was just me and Danny milling around trying to look like we knew what we were doing but the continuous sound of explosions and automatic weapons fire in the distance was adding to our uneasiness.

"Jesus Christ Sal, how the hell did I let you talk me into this nightmare. What do we do if the armored vehicle doesn't come to pick us up?" Danny said with a concerned look.

Looking at my watch I replied, "don't sweat it, the flight for the guys that are leaving doesn't depart for another four hours and ten minutes so they won't be allowed to enter the airport grounds for another ten minutes or so." Pausing and looking around, I added, "They'll be here!" I said with confidence that I didn't really possess.

The parking lot was now void of vehicles except for one lone taxi driver who kept eyeing us as either a potential fare or a kidnapping target with an opportunity to deliver us to insurgents for a hefty bounty. We gave the dude a look of, you better not even think about it.

Out of nowhere a speeding out of control Toyota Hilux pickup truck sped into the parking lot, slamming on his brakes and skidded toward us shattering the quiet in the parking lot. The doors swung open before the vehicle was completely stopped, we didn't know if we should run or get ready to rumble.

Two men jumped out grimed faced and quickly began taking luggage out of the truck. The driver got out of the vehicle and approached us, "Are you the two replacements?"

I responded to his question with mine, "Are you with R.A.P?"

"Yeah I'm with the Rapid Action Company, you Rossi and Mahoney?" he said with a strong British accent.

Danny responded, "Yep, that's us!"

The driver hurriedly commanded us, "Quick shit, load your gear, don your body armor and get your weapons then let's get the hell out of here."

"Why, is there a problem?" inquired Danny.

"Yeah there's a problem, Afghan Police Intelligence put out a BOLO (be on the lookout) for suicide bombers planning to blow themselves up today in or near the terminal!"

We looked at each other with a sudden burst of urgency and quickly started stashing our footlockers and backpacks into the truck and donned our body armor. "Man, oh man, what the hell did I let you talk me into," Danny said for the umpteenth time.

I let out a chuckle but continued getting everything stored, didn't want to get blown up on day one! As we boarded the truck, the two guys we were replacing wished us good luck and warned us to trust no one! We shook hands with them and they quickly started walking to the terminal not uttering another word.

As we departed we realized the Hilux pickup truck was unarmored. "Hey, where's the armored vehicle?" I asked the driver.

"They're all out on missions so when there's an airport run we use whatever's available. Now lock and load your weapons, windows down, keep your heads on a swivel and call out anything suspicious." The second we were loaded, we sped off at a breakneck speed!

During the drive to the team house, the driver began gabbing and introduced himself, "By the way, my name is Freddie, hope you guys know what you signed up for!"

Me and Danny looked at each other with raised eyebrows and smirks, I replied, "Ok Freddie tell us what we signed up for," I said with sarcasm.

Freddie chortled and said, "Yeah they probably never gave you a full briefing on the situation here. Those two blokes who just left, well, they only lasted three months. They raised the white flag after getting shot up by the Taliban. Now the two mates before them ran into a false checkpoint in the Khan Abad District. Turned out what they thought was a police checkpoint was really Taliban dressed in police uniforms. Both men were never seen or heard from ever again. They were presumed dead since the company paid the families the insurance money!"

Danny turned toward me and shot me a worried glance, I nodded in agreement. We said nothing to Freddie and just kept our M4s pointing out the windows.

I sat in the crew compartment and sitting sideways facing my window with M-4 at the high ready while the Danny needing a lot more leg room sat up front riding shotgun with the muzzle of his M-4 poking out his window.

We were making really good time as Freddie was pedal to the metal but within twenty minutes we ran into a U.S. Army convoy on a desolate stretch which slowed us down to a crawl. Freddie attempted to pass the convoy but the rear Humvee turret gunner waived us down, an indication not to pass, Freddie exclaimed, "Damn!"

We had no idea why he was pissed, so Danny asked, "what's the problem?"

"Men, getting stuck behind a military convoy is bad news. Those guys have a bullseye target on them we don't want to be anywhere close to them, this is bad, really bad. I'm going to slow down a bit, let them get ahead."

No sooner had Freddie finished his last words, a blinding flash of white light made us recoil which was followed by a deafening explosion that slammed us into our trucks' interior. IED's had been remotely detonated on the right side the convoy followed immediately by another detonation near the convoy's left side. Bursts of AK-47 and machinegun fire showered the convoy from a mud house village located about two hundred yards on the right side. Several of the convoy vehicles appeared to be damaged but the soldiers in the stalled vehicles were firing back at the insurgents.

Fearing getting trapped and exposed to lethal fire, Freddie screamed, "hang on we're pushing through, light them up with everything you've got." Freddie violently stomped on the accelerator causing the truck to fishtail left then right before pulling out of the spin and regaining its forward momentum but it knocked me and Danny out of our shooting position for a few seconds. Freddie caught up to the rear Humvee and tried to use it to shield us from the fire as much as possible.

We were now right smack in the middle of the kill zone. Danny was first to regain his shooting position and engaged the insurgents while it took me a few seconds to regain my balance, push the selector switch on my Bushmaster M4 on auto then cut loose with automatic bursts at the mud buildings. A roadside bomb detonated a few seconds too late, exploding behind us which caused all of us to duck but we continued firing at the insurgents. After we pushed through I called to Danny, "check yourself, you Ok?"

Danny gave himself a quick look for any blood, "I'm good." Danny looked over Freddie from head to toe and found no blood, "Freddie you Ok?"

"Yeah I'm good" but he was clearly shaken! "

"Sal you looked yourself over?"

"Yeah I'm good!" After a few minutes Freddie settled down enough to call the Tactical Operations Center (TOC) at our team house on the two-way radio and informed them of what occurred. We were advised the medic would be waiting to check us out.

With the expected adrenaline rush flowing through us, we were high-fiving and bantering back and forth just happy to come out of that kill zone alive. Although the incident seemed like it went on forever, the reality was we passed through the gauntlet of death in less than one minute. We loudly asked each other whether we'd hit any of the insurgents or if we'd actual seen any of them. In actuality we hadn't seen shit other than the muzzle flashes emanating from the mud homes. Quickly, the expected adrenaline dump occurred and all of a sudden our muscles ached and we felt exhausted, hence the truck went silent for the remaining forty-five minute drive as we got lost in our own thoughts. I couldn't decide if we survived the brush with death due to luck or by our actions. I stopped thinking about it and just accepted that we got through it alive.

What a way to start our first day in-country I reflected, one day in, three hundred sixty-four to go before completing our contract. Although we'd heard that this country was known as the graveyard of empires, I was absolutely sure as shit that it wasn't going to be ours!

We arrived at the team house in the late afternoon. Our truck snaked around the concrete barriers used to slow down potential vehicle borne suicide bombers (VBIED). We then were able to approach the thick, twin wrought iron gate doors that were about eight feet tall which led into an expansive parking lot court yard. The team house was surrounded by a ten foot high concrete wall with a parapet walkway leading to guard towers at each corner. Our home compound seemed more like a prison but good for keeping the bad guys out while we slept. The team medic, an older looking American who went by the name of Obie, was there waiting on us. Obie made everyone get out and take off their body armor, shirts, pants, boots and socks. We were all lined up in our skivvies, Obie made us turn around slowly as he observed all of us and confirmed no one had an undetected wound. When he was satisfied, he yelled out, "carry on, you'll live to fight another day!" then walked away back to his clinic.

The head Nepalese Security Officer who was standing behind Obie took a few steps forward and greeted us, "Svagata, welcome" with a big friendly grin on his face. The Nepalese put his right hand on his heart and greeted us again, "Assālam Aleikum, my name is Thapa. I am head Nepali guard," he announced in broken English.

We simultaneously greeted him back with the Wa-alaykum As-salām response and shook hands with Thapa. In a genuinely concerned tone, Thapa asked "You sirs Ok, no injuries?"

Danny answered, "We're Ok Thapa, thanks for asking."

Thapa authoritatively motioned with his hand at the six Afghans who were dressed in Khaki tactical uniforms, desert boots and AK47's slung over their shoulders, then in a loud command voice called out to them, "Come here quick, take the men's gear to their room!" The six Afghans immediately ran up to us, stood at attention and saluted. We saluted them back. The Afghans quickly unloaded our gear taking it into the building. Thapa informed us that the six Afghans were a part of our mobile team along with four Nepalese Gurkha supervisors. He assured us not to worry, our gear would be taken to our assigned rooms and nothing would be stolen. We walked over to the pickup truck where Freddie was putting tape on the bullet holes to document the damage. He looked at us and said, "twenty seven holes and not a scratch on any of us, we were very lucky, either of you Irish?"

Me and Danny looked at each other and started laughing at the same time. Danny then replied to his question, "Freddie, great job getting us out of that ambush!" Freddie responded with a smile and a thumbs up but I think he was still shaken and affected by the attack.

With a bit of urgency Thapa called out to us. "Sirs please follow me, the project manager ask me to take you to his office immediately after you arrive."

We followed Thapa into the two story house and into the project manager's office. A man seated by the desk stood up and said, "Welcome, I'm, Mike Rogers the project manager for this contract, please call me Mike. So, a little excitement on the way in, you men Ok?"

I shook hands with him and introduced myself, "Sal Rossi, pleased to me you Mike. We're Ok, I guess that's why we're making the big bucks right?"

Danny stepped up next to me and introduced himself, "Danny Mahoney, please to meet you Mike, a bit of excitement getting here but I'm sure it's not like that every day, I hope."

Mike laughed and replied, "No, not really, please have a seat."

Mike had the look of a man who had lived a martial life. His had a rugged physic, was darkly tanned with dark lines streaking throughout his weather-beaten face and not someone to trifle with. We grabbed a couple of chairs and sat across from Mike. "I've read your police resumes and evaluations during your four week vetting course. You guys did very well during the tactical training."

"Thank you for that sir, the training already has paid off!" replied Danny.

"So, I know quite a bit of you two. Now about me, I'm a retired U.S. Army Colonel, Ranger Battalion, then 5th Special Forces Group, followed by a long stint at the

Pentagon. Retired about sixteen months ago and have been on this project for about a year. I initially hesitated bringing on board a couple of cops for this high threat type project. However, the previous military personnel we selected had their ups and downs so I thought I'd give a couple of tough cops a shot at this gig. I'll tell you what I told the others, if you think a mission is too dangerous you have the right to turn it down, no questions asked by me!

"No worries Mike, you can count on us. We will travel anywhere, anytime!" I replied.

Mike then got down to brass tacks immediately. "Excellent, great to hear that, bottom line men, I'm very busy with administrative matters, meetings at the United Nations compound, the U.S. Embassy and ISAF bases. What that means is, you won't have much interaction with me. You guys are your own bosses and I expect nothing less than 100% professionalism. If you screw up you'll be seeing me in an up close and personal way, you guys follow?"

In unison we both replied, "Yes sir!"

"To the heart of the matter, your job is not complicated but can be extremely dangerous. You'll ferrying people, supplies, food and at times, significant amounts of cash throughout the country to our team houses, all of it, inherently dangerous." While the events are fresh in your mind, go to the TOC and complete a use of force (UOF) report and leave them in my tray. I'll review the reports tonight and let you know if I need additional information. The report is no big deal, one page, mostly fill in the blanks, number of rounds expended, injuries and a short narrative. Freddie will fill his UOF plus the property damage report for the bullet holes in the truck. Alright, I know you guys are dead tired from the long flights and just got into a firefight but there's no rest for the weary on this gig. We have a short fuse requirement for tomorrow. You depart at the crack of dawn for a mission to deliver one-hundred thousand dollars in cash and truck tires to our team house in Mazar-e Sharif . It's a brutal, long ass drive, about ten hours in each direction. Go ahead get your room and gear set up and get some rest." He leaned forward and in a low voice advised, "you two watch your asses, trust the Nepalese but no one else. Get to know those guys, your life depends on it!"

With our heads still spinning, we got up shook hands with Mike and staggered out of his office. Me and Danny took Mike's words as an order so although we were exhausted and hungry we beat feet to the TOC and completed the UOF report. The ammo count for rounds expended in our brief firefight totaled one hundred, ninety-eight rounds, damn! Only a few hours in-country, double damn! Turning toward Danny I muttered, "You know what the strangest thing is of all this?"

"All of it!" Danny said as we headed toward our rooms.

"Agreed but the fact is we just got into a heated gunbattle and the project manager is nonchalant about the entire incident as if this shit happens every day."

"I hope not partner!"

With that we went to the kitchen area for what seemed like the never ending first day of our contract!

4

SALANG PASS, THE TUNNEL OF DEATH

Dum Spiro Spero [While I Breath, I Hope] - Unknown

Our team house had a dining room on the top floor with a huge restaurant sized kitchen. Our food was prepared by a chef who was from India and lived in our team house.

Thapa, our Nepalese chief guard turned out to be a blessing for us. We realized we were starving and hustled upstairs to the dining room to see if we could get an early dinner. Thanks to Thapa the chef was already waiting for us with burgers and fries. No doubt it was the fuel we desperately needed to stabilize us somewhat after crossing several time zones that had completely desynchronized our body clock along with a gunbattle thrown in for good measure!

While chowing down, the ever attentive Thapa stopped in to see how we were doing. We asked Thapa if in the coming days he could buy a few items we needed since our mining gear was still back in the U.S. We drew and described on a piece of paper something resembling our plastic gold pans and a box sifter. To our utter amazement, the following morning Thapa along with the Afghan team members secured two round tubs which actually had grooves around its interior, perfect for panning, along with two shovels and a large bucket with wire mesh which would function as an ad hoc sifter. Thapa was a unique, resourceful individual who throughout our time on the contract greatly supported not only our convoy duties but to a great extent, facilitated our search for gold and gems.

After dinner we went back to our rooms and continued the arduous task of sorting out our personal and tactical gear. As a former Marine I had no problem getting my shit sorted out quickly. I then responded to Danny's room to see how he was coping. I knocked on his door and he yelled to come in. When I walked in, it looked like a lunatic on LSD had rampaged through his room, shit strewn all over the floor.

"Well, looks like you're settling in real nicely, ay Danny."

"Hell, I've got personal gear, tactical gear, what the hell? Actually I was just running through my mind everything that happened on the way here. I tell you Sal, I bet that's the kind of shit storm that made the two guys we replaced quit after only three months on the job."

Although I was a bit rattled myself, I stayed with Danny a couple of hours settling down his nerves and helping him get his room and gear organized.   Before leaving his room Danny thanked me and commented, "Hey, I'm not embarrassed to say, I'm a bit apprehensive. You know we've been through a lot of stuff in the streets of D.C. but man, this is different!, how about you?"

"Look partner, no doubt that was intense and we got out of there with our hind parts intact by the narrowest of margins. You know we got good training before we left and we've got more situational awareness than anybody in this country, not to mention our secret weapon," I reassured him.

"Oh yeah, what's that?"

I picked up his 20 inch, aluminum, fish knockout bat sitting on his bed, "anyone tries any crap with us, we'll bust em up, ay!"

Finally a smile of confidence on the big Irishman's face, "Yeah man" he exclaimed along with a high-five.

The last thing I did that night was email Jean a quick note making sure everything was Ok at home and putting her at ease that me and Danny made it to Kabul without any problems. Of course there was no mention of our little welcome ride from the airport to the team house. It was now 9:00 PM local time but my body was screaming to sleep and not think. I racked out but in what seemed like no more than two seconds later the shrill, ear-splitting sound of my alarm clock brought me back from a dead sleep causing me to jolt up and out of bed. Good grief I said to myself, it's already morning as a crippling headache covered my head which added to my confusion as I absolutely had no idea where the hell I was.

After I regaining my senses and realized where I was, I got dressed quickly then rushed up to the dining room. To no surprise, Danny was already well into his breakfast. As I sat down, he saw fit to take time away from destroying an omelet the size of a football to greet me warmly, "Hey Sal, sembri una merda" [*you look like shit*].

"Hey, don't talk I-talian", we both laughed which was followed by a high-five. I could already tell that today was going to be a great day.

I was really pumped up knowing that on our very first mission we would be travelling through the Salang Pass. The exact location my contact Scott so vividly recounted as having untouched gold veins running through the edges of the river.

Conveniently, our team house was equipped with a massive 500 gallon fueling station. Thapa and his subordinate Nepalese Gurkha, Sejun, had our three armored SUV's fueled up and stocked with food and drinks and ready to roll. Thapa sent the four man Afghan security guards scurrying to our rooms to get our gear which we staged in the hallway per Thapa's instructions.

Before we departed, Danny called out to Thapa, "hey Thapa, we'd like to have a talk with you."

"Sirs of course."

We escorted Thapa around the corner of the building. "You know the makeshift gold pans and sifter you got for us, today we would like to stop somewhere along the Salang river and try them out. Do you have any problems with us doing that?"

Smiling broadly he replied, "No sirs, we follow your orders anywhere, any time."

"How about our Afghan security guards, you think they'll be Ok with this arrangement?" inquired Danny.

"Mr. Danny, the Afghan guards are extremely happy working on this project, they make more money than all of their friends and family members and they get free food at our team house, they never will complain sir!"

I breathed a sigh of relief and informed Thapa, "excellent Thapa, here, take this envelope! There's a $50 dollar bill for you, a $20 for Sejun and $10 dollars for each of the four Afghan security guards. Distribute the money when we stop to do some prospecting! Every time me and Danny prospect we will give you an envelope with money to distribute."

"Sirs, you are most generous! Thank you so much. You can count on me and my men to take good care of you both!" I think the Nepalese Gurkhas would have eagerly gone along with our prospecting plans regardless of any payments from us because these guys were the most incredibly loyal hard workers we had ever come across.

I drove the lead SUV with Thapa, the chief Gurkha guard, as my co-pilot. Danny was driving the SUV behind me with Sejun a secondary Nepalese Gurkha supervisor as his co-pilot and the trailing SUV was occupied by our four Afghan security guards. Me and Danny had M-4's with twenty-five mags each while the Nepalese and Afghan security guards had AK-47's and one M249 (SAW) machinegun.

We went through the radio check procedure and once the third SUV announced he was 'UP' we exited through the tall iron compound gates at exactly 0600 hours!

After a couple of hours we were out of Kabul Province and into Parwan province. Occasionally we encountered an army or police checkpoint where we would flash our American flag placard then slowly roll past their checkpoint without stopping. This tactic worked the majority of times to keep us safe by not opening the doors of our armored SUV and exposing us to anything that could kill us.

The roads we travelled were as big a threat to us as were the Taliban. We encountered a mixture of pothole strewn, semi paved and rough stone thoroughfares that could easily and quickly cripple an armored vehicle or send us careening down a mountainside to a certain death.

So whenever we came across a stretch of smooth paved road we would accelerate to the max to make up for lost time. For some unknown, strange and bizarre reason known only to Afghans, paved roads would have hidden humps that were impossible to detect. So during these stretches we'd punch the accelerator to 50 to 70 miles per hour speeds, however when we drove over the hidden humps, our 8,000 pound armored SUV's would fly up in the air and slam back onto the roadway causing our heads to slam into the roof of our vehicle. Even though I'm only 5' 10" my head still would slam into the truck ceiling causing significant neck pain. However, Danny being 6'4 was really getting the hell beat out of him. With me in the lead vehicle and Danny behind me, I frequently looked in the rear view mirror after hitting a bump just to see Danny's reaction. Funny as shit, Thapa and the other security guards would put their hands over their mouth to hide their laughter out of respect. Invariably Danny would get on the radio cursing up a storm which just made us laugh ever harder.

This being our first mission and basically knowing nothing about how things work, I asked Thapa if there was a AAA type road service to call for assistance should we have a breakdown. You could have sworn I asked him about the possibility of cold water fusion in our lifetime! Basically we had three options, we fix the problem ourselves or we fasten a strap on the disabled SUV and tow it to our destination or call our team house and have our on-call mechanic respond to our location. None of the options were of comfort but that's why we were getting paid the big bucks.

There were food stands here and there but the food was not hygienically safe to eat and for security reasons not advisable for westerners to stop, eat and relax. Thapa had this issue resolved. On all our missions that took us outside of Kabul Province, he arranged with the cook to fill up several coolers with sandwiches and Gatorade type drinks along with two or three cases of water and a case of MRE's in each vehicle.

Once we cleared the main town of Charikar in Parwan Province we entered the Salang District and began the journey further into the interior. It soon became clear that Afghanistan wasn't just a poor country, outside of Kabul City, it was like looking at a pictorial of biblical times, mud home communities with no running water or electricity.

As we pushed further into the Hindu Kush mountain range, looking out the windshield an eerie feeling washed over me as if our vehicles were being swallowed and cut off from the world by the mountains all around us. No matter how many times we made this trip, the same feeling washed over me, I now understood one of the reason why Afghanistan got the nickname, graveyard of empires!

We continued pushing up the Hindu Kush mountain road, heading for the thirteen thousand foot elevation peak. The twisting, winding one lane road, barely the width of a vehicle, had no guardrails to protect us from falling thousands of feet to certain oblivion.

I felt relieved once we arrived at the top of the mountain range only to come face to face with the gaping semi-circle hole entrance to the Salang Pass tunnel, A.K.A. 'the 'tunnel of death'. The tunnel is approximately two miles long and no adjectives exist that can sufficiently describe this terrifying place. Our three vehicle convoy entered the narrow two-lane road which had no overhead lights or ventilation. Thick, putrid black exhaust from heavy duty trucks quickly engulfed my vehicle creating a carbon monoxide death trap in the interior cabin. With nearly zero visibility, we encountered a farmer moving his herd of goats through the tunnel which made the gridlock almost unbearable. The positive side of the gridlock was that we drove over potholes big enough to swallow an M1 Abrams tank at a one foot per hour speed sparing our SUV's from certain damage.

It took over one hour to traverse the two mile apocalyptic, toxic nightmare of a passageway! As soon as we cleared the tunnel I radioed for all vehicles to pull over to the side of the road for a, clear our lungs moment.

As we exited our vehicles, me and Danny were coughing up the nasty toxins stuck in our throats. "Good God Sal, we need to go back into the tunnel!"

"Are you shitting me, why?' "I asked truly disturbed at that probability.

"I think I lost a lung somewhere in there!" as he continued to cough.

I laughed in between my coughing fits. "They should put a sign at the entrance of that hellhole, all hope abandon ye who enter here!"

"Poetic Sal but spot on! How about we look into taking a helicopter to Mazer next time?"

"Good thinking Danny, we'll look into that with Mike for sure when we get back to Kabul." Little did we know that during our time on the contract we would conduct twenty-five round trips through Dante's Inferno! Of course no helicopters for us. We were road warriors!

In what seemed like an eternity later, we reached the bottom of the Salang Pass mountain range with the brakes on our armored SUV's smoking hot. A few minutes later we stopped at an isolated river's edge where my contact Scott had identified as a rich gold ore location but also to cool down the brakes on our vehicles. Once we stopped and staged the vehicles, Afghan and the Nepalese guards took turns providing 360 degree security while the others chowed down. Me and Danny ate quickly then donned water-proof boots and moved to the river with our makeshift pans while Sejun brought our bucket sifter and shovels to the river's edge. After about thirty minutes and getting a feel for our makeshift pans and water conditions, we started to agitate the material as heavy black sand rapidly began sinking gold flakes and small irregular shaped nuggets to the bottom.

I called out to Danny who was about twenty feet from me, "How you doing?"

"Incredible gold flakes and nuggets, you?"

"Same here, amazing!" It soon became clear how pristine Afghanistan was, within a few hours we recovered about an ounce of gold. Panning out that much gold ore in America would take years, pretty much unthinkable where every stream, river and creek had been repeatedly worked by prospectors for a century.

This was only a test of how we were going to operate, so before too long I called out to Danny, "Hey man our time's up, let's move out."

"Copy that."

I radioed Thapa that it was time to depart. Me and Danny were wearing heavy rubber gloves and boots to protect us from the very frigid waters. As I began walking out of the river with pan in hand, I slipped on a mossed covered rock and fell into deeper water up to my chest. I let out a yell that was probably heard all the way in Kabul. Danny laughed heartily but the Nepalese and the Afghans covered their mouths to hide their laughter. Several of the Afghans along with Thapa ran to my location and helped me get out of the river. I had a spare set of BDU's in the truck so I was able to change and drive the rest of the way to Mazār with dry clothes. Before departing I joined in on the amusement and jokingly admonished everyone for laughing at me which caused even more laughter from all.

Overall the first prospecting run turned out well in that we got a decent first score, our security team got a good laugh, a good bonding moment for us all.

Our three vehicles were staged and we proceeded to push on to the Mazār team house. The rest of the trip was bone jarring boredom with one fuel stop on the side of the road where a man displayed a fuel for sale sign. He had a small child who used a rubber hose to fuel up our vehicles from large gas cans as the old man looked on supervising the operation.. Our Afghan security guards paid the man in Afghani currency and we sped off for Mazār.

We arrived at the team house at 5:50 PM, so minus the two hours of prospecting, the 230 mile trip had taken nearly twelve hours. The Mazār team house had the same layout as ours in Kabul, just a much smaller house and compound. We went inside the house to meet the engineer on the contract. Harry was a personable Canadian who seemed content working in a somewhat far flung region and he was all too happy to have us yanks visit just to chat with a westerner.

Our security team immediately unloaded the four Kamaz truck tires and turned them over to the Mazār Afghan security guards. Me and Danny had dinner with Harry then got down to business. We went to Harry's office and plopped down the two large bags containing one-hundred thousand dollars in cash. During our time in Afghanistan all business transactions were conducted in cash, credit cards were a no-go. The cash we brought for Harry to pay the salaries of Afghan workers and for the purchase of contract related materials available in the Mazar area. It took Harry several hours to hand count the money as we looked on. Once he was satisfied of the count, he signed off on our hand receipt for the money and tires. Dead tired from the trip we had a quick meal and beat feet to our own rooms for a solid sleep even though the bed mattresses were as soft as a slab of cement!

The following morning we conducted a security escort for Harry as he checked on the construction progress of a wastewater treatment plant as well as two other infrastructure projects he was responsible for overseeing. Although Harry had his Nepalese and Afghan security guards assigned to him, anytime me and Danny were present at a team house we assumed responsibility for coordinating and managing the security movements outside the compound. Harry served in the Canadian military so he was accustomed to being armed. Oddly, Harry ported a Korean War vintage M-2, full auto 30 cal. carbine with a 30 round mag inserted. Where the hell he got an M-2 and the 30 carbine ammo is anybody's guess. Later me and Danny had a good laugh as we kidded him that he looked like he was on patrol in the Korean DMZ. Harry had an easy going temperament and took the ribbing well.

The next day we said our goodbyes to Harry and his security team then roared out of the compound eager to get back to our team house in Kabul. We stopped at the same location we did our panning but only to eat our sandwiches and get mentally ready for the final push home through the dreaded tunnel of death. The return trip through the tunnel was a nightmarish ordeal once again but this time we traversed the two miles quicker, only having to inhale the toxic fumes for about forty-five minutes.

On the way to Mazar we observed a military junkyard on the side of the road in Parwan Province and made a mental note to stop and check it out on the return trip to Kabul. So as we headed home we pulled over to the military scrapyard for a photo Op. We took the opportunity to take photos of us on top of old Soviet Union T-55 and T-62 tanks, armored troop carriers and military trucks which were rusting away and strewn all about.

As we crossed from Parwan Province into Kabul a big 'Welcome to Kabul' banner was a welcome sight which would greet us on all our return trips back to our home compound. Every time I saw that banner I breathed a sigh of relief knowing that we had returned to a somewhat safe area.

Upon our arrival to our team house we were completely wasted. Thankfully the Gurkhas and Afghans took care of unloading and storing our gear and refueling the vehicles while we went straight to the TOC to complete an end of mission summary report.

I told Danny I'd meet him in the dining room once I submitted to Mike the signed money and tires hand receipt. I met up with Mike in his office and handed him the receipt. "How was your first run?" he inquired in a pro-forma manner.

"Uneventful, no problems Mike. Me and Danny turned the stuff over to Harry. He was glad to get the money and tires."

"How'd you get along with Harry?"

Helluva a nice bloke, he's a bit isolated so he enjoyed our company."

Mike responded with a grin, "Great job, you and Danny are going to fit in real well on this project."

"Thanks boss."

"Alright go get something to eat and get some rest."

"Roger that."

Within fourteen days of our arriving in Afghanistan, we received several packages from home with all our prospecting equipment as well as a bunch of snack foods and winter clothes. During the next few months we conducted numerous convoy movements to near and far locations. We frequently found time to prospect on these missions as well as on our days off. To date, we had sent home about twenty thousand dollars' worth of gold ore but only one small green emerald.

Jean and Becky travelled to the diamond district in New York and sold the emerald for a mere one thousand dollars, hardly the big score we were looking for. Of course the gals made a mini vacation of the business trip by staying overnight and catching the Lion King Broadway show. Oh well, make a little spend a lot, the gals deserved that much for putting up with our antics!

5

KNOCK OUT BATS

As the saying goes, difficult roads often lead to lucrative destinations. Yes, the best scores were yet to come!

June 2003

Sometime in late August we were tasked with a convoy mission to our company's team house in Torkham near the Pakistan border. We were responsible for delivering assorted construction tools and frozen foods to Tim Slade, an engineer who was under contract by our company to oversee the construction of a hydro-power plant and other Afghan power facilities to provide badly needed electricity to many isolated communities in that region of Afghanistan.

Our mission also required us to provide close protection security for Tim as he visited and inspected the construction progress of several sites located in unsecured areas of Mihtarlam in Laghman Province. I wrote the operational order for the convoy then me and Danny briefed Thapa and Sejun who then briefed the Afghan security guards.

The following morning as expected, Thapa had our coolers and drinks prepared and the vehicles fueled and ready to rock. Before our departure Thapa approached us with a concerned look on his face. "Sirs, before we depart I would like to inform you of very important matter, if that's Ok?"

Danny answered, "Go ahead Thapa, what's on your mind?"

"Mr. Danny, Mr. Sal, I want to give you a warning of the American we will be visiting" he said while looking down, hesitating a bit.

"Thapa, go ahead speak freely" I urged him.

"Well, the American, Mr. Tim, he an engineer, very smart man but he also very difficult. He screams at us Nepali for anything. But he treat Afghans much worse, often he pushes and kicks our Afghan security men, it's very, very bad sir. I'm afraid someday Afghan will get angry and open fire and kill us all. Please be careful what you do and say around this man, he very dangerous!"

"Thank you for that information Thapa, we'll be careful but let's get on the road." Thapa walked away fast to ensure the staging of the vehicles was being completed.

"Sal, even if this Tim guy is an asshole, let's just play along with him. We don't want anything separating us from our 12K a month and gold ore!"

"Yep, you're right as always Danny!"

As customary, I drove the lead SUV with Thapa by my side calling out the route in the Urdu language which was understood by our Afghan guards as well as all the Gurkhas. Danny was in the SUV behind me with Sejun as his co-pilot and the four Afghan security guards bringing up the rear in their SUV. During the long, bone jarring drive, I'd occasionally chit-chat with Thapa and at other times jibber jabber with Danny on the two way radio to ease the monotony of another long convoy movement. Intermittently me and Danny would start singing on the two-way radio which utterly befuddled the Nepalese and Afghans as they were used to the strict, regimented radio procedures of the former security operators.

The distance from our compound in Kabul to the team house in Torkham was only about 143 miles. But as we learned during our many convoy missions, predicting how many hours it would take to travel a certain distance was impossible. On this mission it took us six hours to traverse the 143 miles of cratered, treacherous, twisting mountain roads. As if the dangerous mountain road wasn't sufficient to test our nerves, we had to contend with the numerous police checkpoints, thousands of cars and trucks playing a game of chicken as they attempt to pass each other along with the occasional Kutchi nomad tribe herding their flocks of sheep through the roads, certainly tested our mental well-being.

As we passed a spectacular gorge along the Kabul River, I radioed Danny, "Hey, on your left is the grid Scott gave me as a super-hot spot."

"Excellent, let's hit it on the way back to the team house," he replied.

"Done deal!"

A few hours later we arrived at the team house and entered through large metal doors and into the court yard. The compound also had towers like all our outlying compounds except the guards in the towers had PKM machineguns, an ominous sign of how close we were to the lawless Pakistan border.

We were met by Kapoor the on-site Nepalese Gurkha supervisor. He was sharply dressed in a Khaki uniform flanked by several subordinate Afghan security guards. He welcomed us with "Assālam alaykum!" Me and Danny respond in kind.

"Nice to meet you Kapoor!" I replied as we both shook hands with Kapoor.

Kapoor replied, "I'm very happy to meet you both. You two are the new security Chiefs, yes?"

Danny replied, "Yes, we'll be seeing a lot of you and your men!"

"That's very good news, the two chiefs you replaced were very good men but they didn't last long, too dangerous, you know. My team will take your gear to your rooms. Sirs, please follow me, I will take you to meet my boss, Mr. Tim."

We followed Kapoor into the team house and to the entrance of an office where Tim was busy tapping on his laptop. Although the door was open Kapoor knocked on the door and announced our arrival, "Mr. Tim, I have the two new security chiefs sir." Tim rudely ignored him and continued his work. Kapoor shuffled his feet, obviously embarrassed and uneasy at Tim's bad manners.

We grasped this awkward moment and took the initiative to enter the office and introduce ourselves. "Hey Tim, Sal Rossi and my partner Danny Mahoney!"

Without looking up from his laptop, Tim replied, "Guys! I'm working on a real important email, have a seat," as he continued slapping the keys on his laptop. We sat down and shot glances at each other, thinking the same thing, what a rude asshole.

Tim finally finished his email, looked up at us and with a narcissistic air of self-importance put us on notice. "Alright Sal, Danny, let me tell you how things work here. I'm responsible for assisting the Afghan Government in getting a ninety-million dollar hydro power plant completed as well as other projects here in the Torkham region. Every now and then I need to travel to unsecured areas of the province and I'll need you two to manage my security detail, anywhere, any time. When I need you I'll contact Mike in Kabul and you guys get your rear ends up to my compound. So that's it. I depart tomorrow at 0700 hours to inspect several sites, when I walk out of this building I expect to see the vehicles staged and the security team fully kitted and ready to roll. Kapoor will get you situated and fed, see you in the morning." With that warm fuzzy greeting Tim got up and walked out of the office.

It was such an over-the-top spectacle that as soon as Tim was out of sight, Danny let loose with some I-Talian insult, "porca miseria, que stronzo! [Damn, what an asshole]

I glanced at Danny, "You're scaring me brother, you're becoming more Italian than me!" We stayed in Tim's office for a few minutes bantering and laughing at Tim all the while Kapoor listened with a look of terror in his eyes.

As we exited Tim's office, Danny said in a serious tone, "that dude definitely has an exaggerated case of self-importance but let's not mess with him. We're here to make the money and get home alive, right?"

"Agreed partner but he still needs to be tuned up!" I opined.

The following morning we had a five vehicle convoy fully staged and ready to roll with all the needed supplies that Tim required. Sure enough, at 0700 hours Tim exited the building with his nose up in the air, not even a good morning to anyone. He briskly walked to the third SUV as if he were a Head of State and on cue his Afghan security guard who was waiting by the vehicle, opened the passenger door as he got in without uttering a word. Tim could be seen pulling out what appeared to be construction blueprints and spreading it out on the bench seat .The Afghan security guard quickly closed the door which was the signal for all of us to mount up and depart.

We went through the whole radio routine making sure all drivers and security personnel were 'UP' and ready to roll. As soon as the fifth vehicle radioed he was UP, I ordered the lets roll order and we launched out of the compound. The long boring journey took us through crowded, little towns, then to the hydro power plant which was deep into the countryside. Then there it was in the middle of nowhere, a ginormous power plant with a parking lot rivalling Disney Land in Orlando. As we staged the vehicles, we dismounted in an impressive, coordinated manner and everyone moved to their designated protective positions as Tim got out of his vehicle. Everything was looking very good, I thought!

It's essential during close protection walking formations that security personnel continually adjust their position relative to the protectee. It's an art that has to be practiced repeatedly, if not, things can go sideways pretty quickly and of course this time it did. During our box protection formation around Tim he suddenly turned left and bumped into Hamid, our Afghan security guard who was in the left side position. Shit like this happens, not the end of the world but to Tim it was a big deal, he angrily shoved Hamid and yelled at him, " Keep your damn distance!" He then turned to us and bellowed, "You guys better fix this clown show!"

Even though our blood was boiling, we bit our tongues as we both realized this was not the place or time to address Tim's lack of proportionality to Hamid's mistake, so we gave Tim a thumbs up and a nod. Tim met up with a few European and Afghan counterparts then walked into the hydro-power plant office. Before we moved our guys to their static posts around the power plant, we summoned everyone for a quick meeting.

I started first, "I want to tell you that I'm very happy with everyone's performance so far, Danny go ahead let em know."

"As Sal said, keep up the good work guys, keep your heads on a swivel and keep your distance from Mr. Tim. There was no reason for him to yell and push Hamid." Speaking directly to Hamid, Danny continued, "Me and Sal deeply apologize for Tim's actions, we promise we will talk to him about this!" Hamid and the rest of the Afghans looked very pleased at our words.

Hamid replied, "Thank your sirs!" with a big grin on his face.

Tim concluded his business at the hydro-power plant and we convoyed to three other sites all without any further hiccups. Upon our arrival at the Tokham team house the Head of Sate comedy show continued. Tim exited his vehicle and entered the building without even a thank you! Me and Danny huddled up by our vehicles and thinking out loud he uttered, " man forget what I said yesterday, this asshole seriously needs an immediate attitude adjustment!"

"Don't worry, tomorrow morning he's gonna get a come-to-Jesus moment," I replied.

"Definitely," Danny said.

We asked Thapa to rally up our security guys and the Torkham guards for an after-action briefing before everyone split up to complete the post mission cleaning and refueling of vehicles and myriad of other chores. As soon as everyone was present we informed the group of our plan that during the next few months we would be coming to Torkham and conducting extensive VIP close protection and firearms training which was very well received by both the Afghan and Nepalese guards. We told them that both of us were very impressed on our first mission with them and that we plan to inform the project manager in Kabul that we were very pleased with their professional performance.

With brimming smiles the Afghan and Nepalese guards raised their AK47's in the air and spontaneously yelled "Taschakor!, Taschakor!" [*Thank you, thank you*]

After the meeting me and Danny were still fuming at Tim's negligent and dangerous conduct. Besides violating basic standards of management like not disciplining a subordinate in front of his colleagues, this dude had absolutely no situational awareness. The green-on-blue attacks in Afghanistan were becoming common place wherein Afghan police officers, soldiers or security guards, for the slightest reason, would open fire and kill American and European personnel.

We finished the evening with a good meal prepared by the team house cook but we agreed that Tim's day of reckoning had arrived and an extreme invasion of his personal space was warranted.

The following morning me and Danny got our gear into our SUV's and prepared to depart for Kabul. I looked at Danny and said, "I think it's time to have a nice chat with Mr. Tim!"

"Definitely. Bats?" Danny responded with a determined look.

"Yep, bats for sure!" I said.

Just like in our cop days when we ported a wooden Baltimore Bomber baton which had a humongous wooden knob on the tip in case someone broke bad. Here in Afghanistan we kept the aluminum bats in our vehicles as essential gear, for just in case moments. We retrieved our bats from the trucks and proceeded back into the team house in search of Mr. Tim. We walked with a definite purpose to our step and were so focused with our fury that we walked past Afghan and Nepalese guards without greeting them which probably alerted them that some serious shit was about to go down.

We located Tim in his office as always tapping away on his laptop and shuffling papers. We entered his office and closed the door behind us, holding the bats behind our backs, I called out to Tim, "Hey Tim, we just wanted to stop by and say goodbye."

Tim looked up, with an annoyed look on his face and replied, "Alright, goodbye, see you next time!"

I quickly replied, "Not quite Timmy me boy."

Tim looked up with a scowl, "What the hell do you want?"

Danny quickly jumped in, "Hey man, we're sensible guys so we can make allowances for your shitty temperament but we're not going to put up with the way you treat our Nepalese and Afghan security guards."

Clearly pissed, Tim's eyebrows curled against each other, and his eyes enlarged. He stood up and seethed, "First off, the Afghans and Nepalese security guards working here are under my command not yours!"

I immediately interrupted him, "Technically yes but we are the security chiefs so the training and welfare of every security man working on this contract, and that includes your men, are solely our responsibility."

Danny chimed in, "During the past two days we got a good look at your oversight of the Afghan security guards, there's just no excuse for not only embarrassing the guard in front of everyone but you actually physically shoved him, do you realize . ."

Tim stood up, walked to the front of his desk and loudly interrupted Danny, "You two are out of line and looking for a one way ticket back to America. You better back off right now and get your rookie asses back to Kabul before you really piss me off!"

I motioned to Danny with a nod of the head and he knew exactly what to do. I revealed the aluminum bat that I had hidden behind my back. I stepped forward crowding Tim while Danny encircled him from the rear and for the first time Tim did not look so confident. I quickly shoved Tim's chest with the tip of the bat. Tim tried to step backwards but he bumped right into the gigantic Danny who shoved Tim forward with the tip of his Bat.

With a clenched jaw Danny egged him on, "Go ahead Timmy, get pissed."

Our aggression rocked Tim's worldview who was now blinking his eyes rapidly and trying to steady himself. In a loud voice I put him on notice, "Hey Tim, you got it wrong, it's us who are pissed and this is how it's going to be here on in! You're going to act in a professional manner, from this day forward you'll treat both the Nepalese and the Afghan guards with respect, you got that?"

By now, a large contingent of Nepalese and Afghan security guards had been alerted to what was happening and congregated just outside Tim's door eavesdropping.

They reacted with enormous glee of what they were hearing.

While Tim had turned to look at Danny, Sal grabbed Tim's shirt in the chest area while Danny simultaneously grabbed the back of Tim's shirt collar.

Inside of me was a thunderstorm waiting to explode but I knew our response had to be proportional. I finished Tim's Come to Jesus moment by telling him in a firm and loud voice, "You better fix yourself mister! By the way, we don't give a shit who you complain to either!"

No further action was needed, Tim was visibly shaken and his normal confident air of superiority had vanished. Being completely overwhelmed he fully submitted and uttered something unintelligible and nodded his head so we released our hold on him and he stormed out of his office.

The group of Nepalese and Afghan security men who were eavesdropping scrambled away from the door in order to avoid Tim knowing they were listening in on his butt whooping!.

As we walked toward the courtyard Danny asked, "What do you think he'll do now?"

"What the hell can he do, call the cops?" I replied. We both laughed at the prospect of the Afghan police conducting an investigation and wind up arresting Tim for mistreating the Afghan guards.

As we exited the house we saw Kapoor was waiting for us along with a contingent of the guard force. With a broad grin on his face he said, "Sirs, I along with my team would like very much to shake your hands before you depart." Thapa who was standing next to us whispered that the entire Torkham team was aware of what transpired in Tim's office. Of course we complied and walked up and down the lined guards and shook hands with all. Occasionally one of the guards would give us a hug and shower us with thank you's. When we finished Kapoor stated, "I speak for all, we thank you for everything you have done for us sirs, we your friends for life!"

We departed the team house and began our journey back to our home in Kabul with a prospecting pit stop at the Kabul River. A couple hours later I asked Thapa to get on the radio and advise the other two vehicles to get ready to exit the roadway. Our three vehicle convoy pulled off the road and followed the GPS directional arrows that took us through a narrow gravel path by the river's edge.

Looking down at my GPS I called out, "Whoa this is the spot, Thapa let the other vehicles know to stage right here," I said while scanning the area. This spot was such an inhospitable area for human habitation, I wondered how the hell Scott found the opportunity to come to such an isolated area. Our Afghan security men unloaded the mining equipment and once we had everything ready they fanned out in a 360 security posture around me and Dann as we began panning the riverbed.

Within the hour there was the shout of gold, shimmering yellow everywhere as the richness of this spot became more evident. We started recovering not only flakes but an impressive number of gold nuggets in our pans which were shaking from our trembling excited hands.

This war torn country was a nightmare but it contained unbelievable mineral riches waiting to be tapped. Me and Danny were just scraping off the top layer of unspoiled virgin lands where gold, silver and precious gemstones have been lying in the shallows for an eternity.

I decided to let Danny keep panning while I moved further up the river where I noticed an outcropping of rocks flashing mineralization. I gouged out a small fragment from the bluish quartz vein and hot damn, it was almost pure gold! I got on my radio and told Danny to come to me ASAP.

Danny ran the hundred yards to my location and excitedly blurted out, "what?"

I showed him the chunk I had chiseled out, "Look at this shit."

"Whoa" he said with widened eyes.

"There's a lot more where that came come from," as I showed him the rich vein.

"Hot damn, I think we've found a motherlode, I'm beginning to believe all your scheming might just pay off!"

"Right on," I said as we celebrated with high-fives.

We labored relentlessly but lost tract of time until Thapa warned us that dusk was fast approaching.

"Sal, let's start putting our gear away and beat feet before the Taliban vampires come out."

"Sounds good, you know if we keep making hauls like this we might have to extend our contract for another twelve months, ay partner?"

Danny didn't say a word and just shot me a stare of daggers.

Soon enough we packed our stuff back into the SUV's and departed for home. Three hours later we arrived at our team house totally and completely exhausted but ecstatic at our very successful prospecting.

While unpacking our gear Mike called out to us waving his hand for us to come. As we approached he inquired, "Hey guys how'd it go?"

Without missing a beat Danny replied, "All went very well boss, the Torkham security team performed very well."

With an inquisitive look on his face, Mike asked, "So the Torkham team and you guys getting along like one big happy family?"

Mike's probing question alerted me that he already knew what had gone down so I made direct eye contact with him and replied, " I think so boss, I really do!"

Mike shot a shrewd look at us, nodded his head, "Ok, carry on men" and promptly walked away without saying another word which we assumed was tentative approval of our conduct.

We looked at each other and Danny uttered in cautionary tone, "Phew, a close call partner but I think we're alright."

"Yep, I think so too."

There was no doubt that Tim had already called Mike and demanded we be removed from the contract. We attributed Mike's support to his knowledge of Tim's reputation as a detached, rude asshole, who regularly mistreated his Afghan and Nepalese security guards.

As a postscript, our relationship with Tim took an unpredictable but positive turn. From that day forward, neither me, Danny nor any member of the security team assigned to the Torkham compound ever had a problem with him again. During our eight months on the contract we made numerous trips to escort Tim all over that region, of course always finding time to prospect. In fact, anytime we visited Torkham we brought Tim a bottle of bourbon or scotch as a peace offering and we actually shared a few laughs together before all was said and done. We never again had to put out fires with his Afghan and Nepalese security guards who were re-invigorated and able to concentrate on more important things like staying alive during convoy mission and home life issues.

Another postscript to the Torkham area, my guesstimate is that this location yielded more than half of the two-hundred forty ounces of gold we eventually recovered. I lamented that our time in Afghanistan was limited and that instead of us, some entrepreneurial Afghan someday was going to be extremely wealthy mining this location

6

CONVOY MISSIONS, PROSPECTING & THE DREADED NDS

*Don't stop when you're tired, stop when you're done. –
Unknown*

Although we had high hopes of striking it rich in the untapped gold fields of Afghanistan, keeping people and materials safe was our overriding obligation, prospecting was only an extra-curricular activity. During the ensuing five months we continued to prospect for gold and gemstones without it ever affecting the delivery of supplies or conducting close protection operations. The Surobi river location, where we struck the rich vein constantly yielded eye popping chunks of quartz shot full of gold. Typically we'd crush the quartz with a hammer, grind them up as best as possible then put it into our gold pans, add water and expose the gold ore. Gemstones were a lot more elusive but we did locate a few hot spots in the riverbeds where we got a few nice finds of emeralds, rubies, along with green, blue and pink tourmaline.

We continued to ship anything and everything home that looked like gold and precious gems which usually turned out to be the real deal as our wives would confirm in code language. Our wives created separate LLC trading companies and very smartly sold the gold and gems then split the proceeds under their company name.

Mike was the type of supervisor who was seldom seen but knew what his subordinates were doing at any given time of the day or night, truly an art form! I believe that Mike had an inkling of our prospecting activities but he never inquired about it. Surely the fact that we weren't slackers and typically put in fourteen to sixteen hour days except for Fridays which was the Sabbath for Afghans and basically the entire country closes down.

On work days when there were no outbound convoy missions we would either conduct live fire training using the nearby mountains as a backstop or close quarter combat and hostage rescue tactics training. We were certain that Mike observed our hard work plus the fact that we never turned down a mission regardless of danger. In fact, some of the unsecured regions we travelled, not once did we see another American or European security operator. All this was not lost on Mike who was very proud of his team since managers from other State Department projects would request his assistance in moving supplies and people in extremely dangerous parts of the country which I'm convinced contributed to Mike not prying into our extracurricular activities.

Our responsibility was not relegated to transporting people and materials on convoy missions. We had full responsibility for providing security for our team house and ensuring that our static Nepalese and Afghan security guards were mission capable of repelling any attempts to overrun our complex which had occurred at other expatriate housing compounds in Kabul. We were of the mindset that we needed to continually train for the worst case scenarios consequently we put our Nepalese and Afghan security guards through the same tactical training we underwent during our vetting course in the Carolinas.

This continuous training was put to the test one late night. I am a very light sleeper whereas Danny could sleep through a ten megaton nuclear detonation. One night at just past midnight I heard the crackle of automatic gunfire. With barely my eyes open I jumped out of bed and quickly inserted my feet into the desert boots which were always pre-staged for any emergency. I grabbed my M4 and ammo pouch with ten mags and ran towards the TOC on the ground floor of our four level house. I immediately bumped into Thapa who was already fully kitted up with weapon and ammo bandoliers. He blurted out, "Sir, Camp Fletcher is under attack by Taliban." Camp Fletcher was only a hundred plus yards from our compound. I ordered Thapa to get the security team deployed to their pre-arranged defensive positions while I searched for Danny. By the time I reached Danny's room he was coming out fully kitted and we proceeded to get all the expats to the ground level safe room. Although these expats carried sidearms, I posted Sejun and one Afghan guard outside the safe room for a just-in-case scenario.

Once I was satisfied that all the expats were accounted for and in the safe room, we ran up the stairs to the roof where the gunbattle was ongoing and visible. We conducted a radio check with all the static positions making sure the guards were on station with all the ammo and water needed in case of a long siege. The entire event lasted about an hour, which involved a fierce exchange of gunfire with U.S. forces, illuminating the dark night with red and green tracer like a 4th of July celebration. The dumb bastard Taliban's plan was to overrun the security personnel at the front access control gate of the base then self-detonate their explosive vests inside the soldier's sleeping quarters. All the insurgents were killed in the roadway or near the front gate, not one made it pass the delta barrier. The gun battle thankfully did not spill over to our compound but Mike and the other expats were very impressed with our security team's quick and skillful deployment to their assigned positions and getting all the westerners to the safe room.

We communicated regularly with our wives but never shared with them the close calls we'd had. Danny and me agreed that it would serve no purpose to tell them anything that would cause them to worry and lose sleep. Some of our close calls, besides the gunbattle on the very first day of our arrival, included two separate occasions where suicide bombers in a vehicle, known by the acronym VBIED, passed our three vehicle convoy and self-detonated into a U.S. military convoy ahead of us. The explosion on both occasions lifted our eight thousand pound truck into the air. It was extremely heartbreaking to witness the resulting carnage which is beyond description and really hit home the futility of the U.S. mission in this shitty nation. As far as I was concerned, it was an ill-defined mission with vague rules of engagement leading to dead and wounded young Americans, and to what end? Extremely frustrating and sad to see, it still pisses me off so many years later!

One of our immense frustrations was dealing with the Afghan police forces while running the roads. However dealing with the so called secret police, the dreaded National Directorate of Security (NDS) presented a whole lot more headaches and danger. To simply describe those folks as thugs, doesn't really reflect how purposely obtuse and corrupt this outfit was. Whenever we approached an NDS checkpoint we either turned around and attempted to find a different route or if unavoidable we'd press on and interact with them in a polite manner regardless of their thuggish demeanor. These uniformed goons didn't care that their tactics at checkpoints caused massive traffic gridlock so long as they could pilfer some bounty from locals but they really salivated at screwing with westerners. NDS units were notorious for delaying western security convoys for hours and sometimes impounding equipment or armored vehicles which had happened to many mobile security teams.

One early morning we departed on a mission to deliver fifty thousand dollars cash to our team house in the town of Saraj, Parwan Province. As we were exiting Kabul Province, I noticed a checkpoint ahead manned by officers from the NDS. Since this was the only available road to our destination I radioed the two vehicles behind me, "NDS checkpoint ahead, let's go through, have all your papers ready."

The crackle on the radio from the other two vehicles was immediate, "Damn, just what we needed," was Danny's exasperated response.

The response from the Afghan guards in the third vehicle quickly followed, a long thirty second diatribe in their Dari language. I asked Thapa, "What the hell they saying?"

Thapa's reply was priceless, "Boss, they say NDS bad."

I rolled my eyes and replied under my breath, "No shit!" As I rolled up to the checkpoint, the NDS officers asked for many things. We complied and answered all their questions by providing our U.S. State Department ID's, identifying our company and revealing our destination to our team house in the city of Saraj. This should have been sufficient for us to be waived through but it became clear that this group was intent on taking something from us

The officer in charge of the checkpoint ordered me and Danny to step out of our SUV's so we knew there was going to be some serious ball busting. The supervisor demanded to see our weapons manifest which all security companies doing businesses in Afghanistan were required to file quarterly with the Ministry of the Interior. We provided the manifest and his men checked every M4, AK-47 and Glock 9mmm handgun we had which revealed all weapons were correctly listed on the document.

However during their search of our SUV they discovered the two bags containing the fifty thousand dollars cash. The officer in charge demanded to see a bank letter proving the money was related to business operations and not drug transactions money. Of course that type of letter was non-existent and we knew that he knew that, which was irritating the shit out of me and Danny. We bit our tongues and informed him we did not have a bank letter. The supervisor promptly said that his men were confiscating the money but that we could continue on to Saraj.

As his men began removing the bags of cash I unslung my M4 brought it to low ready position. Danny and the rest of our team followed my lead as I informed the supervisor, "Bullshit you ain't taking that money" Our guys fanned around the vehicles attempting to take whatever cover was available.

The NDS supervisor was unaccustomed to this type of push back from westerners, incensed he began yelling commands at his men in Dari. A shitload of NDS officers with AK-47's surrounded our vehicles and aimed their weapons at us. Soon after an NDS pickup truck with an old Soviet Union 12.7mm anti-aircraft machinegun mounted in the bed suddenly screeched to a halt in front of me and Danny. This type of aggressive movement by NDS personnel triggered the civilian occupants of vehicles at the checkpoint to bail out of their vehicles and run for cover on the side of the road for what they were sure was an impending exchange of gunfire.

The NDS supervisor once again yelled something in Dari resulting in the officer manning the anti-aircraft machinegun to yank on the charging handle and put that massive gun into battery with an intimidating loud metallic clanking sound. One slip of the officer's wrist would result in shredding us into little pieces.

Danny confidently told the supervisor, "You can point all the weapons you want but **w**herever that money goes we go!"

The supervisor now clearly beside himself and not sure what to do with the impasse replied, "Ok, have it your way, we're taking all your weapons and we escort you to our headquarters to resolve this problem!"

Danny turned toward me, "Whaddya think, we give up the weapons and live to fight another day?"

As I looked around I couldn't think of any way out of this trick bag so I replied to Danny's question, "Yep, no options at this point" I instructed Thapa to order our men to download their weapons and hand them over to the NDS. Although our Afghan security guards were unhappy, it was the Nepalese guards who were extremely concerned and warned me and Danny to at least maintain possession of our sidearms in case things went sideways. We tried negotiating to keep our sidearms but we were not in a position of power because on this day the NDS were holding all the good cards.

The NDS boxed us in with two of their trucks in front of my vehicle and three NDS trucks behind our third vehicle, then escorted us at gunpoint to NDS Headquarters.

We entered the heavily fortified compound and we staged our vehicles according to the officers' direction. Our Nepalese and Afghan security personnel were detained by our SUV's by heavily armed NDS officers while me and Danny were escorted to another location. On a positive note we were able to negotiate leaving the two bags of cash in our vehicle under the watchful eyes of our security team. As we departed we gave our team members a thumbs-up of confidence that everything would be fine. I got to admit it was mostly an act because my heart was slamming against my chest so hard I thought it would break my ribs as I contemplated what horrors might befall us.

We followed the man into the building and I was half expecting to see a Spanish Inquisition room with whips, chains and other torture devices. However, to our surprise we were ushered into a sprawling, palatial office that had inlayed onyx, hickory wood walls, teak wood flooring, huge crystal chandeliers and high end leather and wood furniture. The plain clothes officer instructed us to have a seat while he stood rigidly as if someone important was due to come in. Me and Danny were looking around and suffering from sensory overload. We waited about fifteen minutes before a heavy set man in a suit walked in, resulting in the plain clothes officer snapping to attention. They exchanged a few words in Dari and the plain clothes officer sat on a chair opposite from us.

In very good English the man identified himself as Abdul-Azim, a regional director of the NDS. Abdul-Azim was all smiles and he apologized for the delay in our movement. He stated that his office had already confirmed who we were and that the money issue had been resolved. He insisted that we have a meal with him to make up for this 'most unfortunate' event. Me and Danny of course accepted his overture, it certainly was an offer we were in no position to refuse. We had a decent conversation and a few laughs with whoever this man was then excused ourselves and got the hell out of that office and back to our vehicles with our stash of cash totally intact!

When we returned to our vehicles, the NDS officers immediately returned our weapons and ammo. Before departure we conducted a quick inventory of our equipment and realized that three fully loaded AK-47 magazines, two fully loaded Glock 9mm magazines, one large bayonet type knife and several MRE meals were missing. The team wanted to confront the NDS officers but I had a mission to complete so I told the guys to forget about that it and get the hell out of here! It was now late in the afternoon but we pushed hard to the team house in Saraj, dropped off the money, then turned and burned back to Kabul.

Upon our arrival to the team house we completed an incident report describing the entire incident which included the amount of ammunition and other items that NDS officers failed to return to us. We briefed Mike, who used our report to shoot emails outbound to the U.S. Embassy. Subsequently, State Department officials had been in contact with our company and informed them that they were extremely impressed by R.A.P. contractor's professionalism and commitment to the U.S. Department of State contract goals.

A few days later Mike forwarded several emails from Rapid Action executives who highly commended Mike and his team for looking after the company's best interest! The emails concluded with, job well done and to expect end of contract bonuses for all involved.

Shit, we just kept winning and thought it would last to the very end but there were storm clouds brewing!

7

TROUBLE

Fata viam invenient. [Fate will find a way]. Virgil

Late **November** 2003

It was Thursday and an unusually warm November night. Our chef decided to serve an incredible lamb dinner on the roof top with Tiki torches illuminating the tables on this windless, spectacular night. We meandered up to the roof early before the other team members arrived so that we could eat and talk about tomorrow's outing on our day off.

Fridays are unique days in Afghanistan; it's the Sabbath, a day of worship so government offices and most shops, big and small, close throughout the country. So for the most part, all Embassies from the international coalition forces stand down with little to no business conducted nation-wide.

The food was already set out on a buffet table and straight away I could tell my partner seemed preoccupied.

"What's up man, everything Ok at home?"

"Ah, yeah, all good" he paused looking away, "Man we've been doing so damn good, I don't know, I'm getting a bad feeling about tomorrow."

"Like what?" I asked.

"Just a premonition I guess but look, we've sent home a shit load of gold and gems without a hiccup, maybe we should quit the prospecting while we're ahead and just finish out our contract?"

I looked around pensively and in a hushed voice said, "You know I didn't want to say anything but the last few days I've had this overwhelming foreboding feeling, hell, so much so that it's turning into a five-boding feeling!"

Danny chuckled at my poor excuse for humor but replied, "Why'd you wait till now to tell me?"

I shrugged my shoulders and said, "Let's do this, tomorrow we'll travel to Dowshi as planned. Do a little prospecting, get a shit load of nuggets, enjoy the clean mountain valley air and end our prospecting with a bang. Look, we've been to Dowshi a bazillion times, locals are friendly and there's nothing there for the Taliban, whaddya think?"

With an apprehensive look he replied, "Alright one last time, what can go wrong, right?"

I nodded and said nothing. I think we both had no appetite and just wanted to get something in our bellies. Out of nowhere a cold breeze started blowing, making our Tiki torches flicker ghost like prowling creatures all around us. We looked up and around and my bravado evaporated, "Hey Danny, let's get the hell off the roof!"

"Agreed!" With that we both retreated to our rooms and locked doors for good measure like frightened school kids!

Needless to say neither one of us got any sleep that night however, we decided to go ahead with our drive to Dowshi, ignoring our gut feelings which had kept us alive and out of serious trouble for twenty-five years on the police force. Thapa, as normal, staged our three armored vehicles along with our prospecting equipment while still dark outside. All the while trying not to attract a attention from other team members who, on their only day off, were most likely sleeping off a drunk from Thursday night partying.

Since this would be our last prospecting trip we both decided to triple the cash for all the guards and instructed Thapa to dole out the money before we departed. What the hell, these guys stuck with us every step of the way and merited a bonus.

As we approached our vehicles everyone had a big smile on their face, no doubt due to a little bit of extra cash in their pockets. I looked at Danny and said, "Let's play it safe today ay boy?"

"Aha, let's do it!"

At zero dark thirty, we alighted through the metal doors of our sanctuary and onwards to Baghlan Province. Although I was in a somber mood, as soon as we were on the road a burst of good vibes hit me. This was a glorious time to be working as a security contractor in Afghanistan. We had the liberty to drive anywhere, anytime. It was just a great deal of freedom that disappeared a few years later when the Afghan Government imposed driving and other restrictions for western security companies and the State Department enacted additional draconian rules and procedures for security operators.

We convoyed through the relatively empty roads for about two hours. The radio chatter between our vehicles was sparse with little joviality. I restricted talk with my co-pilot Thapa to nothing more than warnings of upcoming turns, slow downs, potholes and or debris in the roadway that needed to be relayed to the SUV's behind us.

We arrived at the town of Dowshi where we had made significant finds in the past. We drove off the paved road and about two hundred yards into the river's edge.

We staged our three vehicles in semicircle as usual. In fact by now we didn't have to say anything to the team, everyone knew what to do and where to post up to. The security guards quickly assumed their posts, keeping an eye on things while Thapa and Sejun walked about supervising and keeping a 360 degree surveillance of the area.

This area was not only rich in gold but it had to be one of the most magnificent vistas on the planet. Across the river were high cliffs that glowed a shiny gold-copper color when the sun hit it. Its' sides scarred with ridges of walking paths probably made thousands of years ago. Below the cliffs was a mud village with no electricity and had probably changed very little since 1000 B.C.

Today we were just going to play around the river and try to dig out gems and maybe some nuggets. We had a sifter and shovels and concentrated in an area previously untouched by us. After a few hours of scooping the soil in the shallow river we came up with a few sizeable green tourmaline gems which was good enough to end it right there. We were beginning to breathe easy and ready to kick back at the rivers' edge with sandwiches and trash talk.

We were sitting around thinking about nothing in particular and just listening to the guards bantering back and forth when out of the blue, the tranquility of this remote spot was shattered by the crack of gunfire which caused us to snap up to attention. Me and Danny were caught off guard momentarily as we looked on the flurry of our security guards running and screaming as they tried to figure out where the gunfire was incoming from.

Instinctively me, Danny and Sejun, who was carrying the PKM machine gun, ran for the nearest cover behind the third SUV. Qasim ran behind the second SUV while Thapa and all the others ran behind the first SUV. As soon as Qasim reached the SUV he began firing his AK wildly at the upper side of the hill across the river. He was close enough to us to hear me shout and gesticulate my arms at him, "Qasim!, what the hell you shooting at?" in his excitement he rattled off a long response in Dari which probably translated to, I have no idea what I'm shooting at but maybe my rounds will hit something.

By now a few of the other Afghan guards behind the first SUV began firing sporadically at the hillside but appeared not to have the actual whereabouts of the shooter's location. Although we were civilian contractors, we were required to adhere to the same use of deadly force doctrine as U.S. military personnel. During our four week vetting course instructors continually beat into our heads the legal requirement for engaging enemy fighters with our weapons which was a formula, HA or HI + PID. Another words, if you have either a Hostile Act (HA) or Hostile

Intent (HI) by a bad guy and you have Positive Identification (PID), then you can light him/them up!

Me and Danny retrieved our backpacks from the SUV, took out binoculars and intermittently bobbed up and down from behind the armored SUV as we scanned the hillside trying to figure out exactly who was shooting and from where. The incoming fire was very sporadic as if someone with bad aim was taking potshots at us just for the hell of it. Danny turned toward me with a scowl and yelled out, "Is this the bang you wanted to end the day with?"

I just shook my head and laughed at the irony and returned my focus to where the shots were coming from.

"How many you think Sal, maybe two, three?"

"Hard to say, I don't see jack, we need to sort this shit quick, we've got civilians in the line of fire!"

All of a sudden a rocket propelled grenade flew over our heads making a hissing sound, exploding fifty yards to our rear. We ducked and cringed, "Damn these guys are serious, we'd better do something," Danny yelled out.

I bobbed up quickly and spotted a group of fighters on the lower right side of the hill, one of them attempting to reload his RPG launch tube. I instructed Sejun to mark the spot by sweeping his PKM into their location. As soon as Sejun began blasting the hillside with his PKM, I stood up, pointed to the right side of the hillside and screamed at our guard force to concentrate their fire on that spot. We now got into the fight as we turned the selector switch 180 degrees on our M4's to the auto function and began firing long controlled bursts as our magazines emptied in a matter of seconds. The noise of the gun fire was deafening since we didn't have time to stick our foamy plugs into our ears. I periodically looked around and it seemed like our team was getting ankle deep in empty magazines and spent brass. For sure, our fire was effective as we saw several of the bad guys tumble down the hill.

I assumed that our counter attack had convinced the insurgents to scoot and seek easier targets but it wasn't our day to shine. Events took a dramatic turn for the worse when we heard the dreadful roar of another RPG rocket launch which struck the front end of our second SUV. Boiling hot clouds of black smoke, shrapnel and debris spewed into our position. As the smoke cleared we saw Naji sprawled on his back, out in the open with no cover.

Although we were now taking a more disciplined and sustained automatic weapons fire from the insurgents, I instinctively grabbed the first aid kit out of the SUV and told Sejun to put a fresh belt in his PKM and cover me and Danny while attempted to get Naji out of the line of fire and tend to his injuries. "Danny, ready?"

"Ready!"

"We're moving Sejun."

He replied loudly, "Go, move!" Sejun sprayed the hillside with a two-hundred round burst of suppressive fire, emptying his belt as we sprinted in a zig zag pattern to Naji's location.

As soon as we reached Naji's position I prayed he wasn't dead but there was no time for a cursory medical assessment since we were in the kill zone as rounds whizzed and pinged all around us like a hailstorm. In the meantime Sejun had already reloaded his PKM and was again chewing up the hillside along with our other team members who were tearing up the hillside with bursts of covering fire. With the good covering fire from our guys we grabbed Naji's broomstick, skinny assed-body and ran at a breakneck speed back to the relative safety of our SUV.

Breathing heavily from the sprint and stress, Danny asked in a wheezing tone, "Naji, can you hear me?" Naji shook his head in affirmation.

He was responsive which was good so we immediately began checking from head to toe for wounds. After a cursory assessment I told him with a forced smile, "you're gonna be fine. It's just a few cuts. We'll get you fixed up, OK?"

Naji was breathing heavily with fear, bleeding from lacerations to his face and arms, and groaning but managed to eek out a response, "OK boss, thank you."

We continued bandaging lacerations to Naji's face and arm while the rest of the team continued engaging the insurgents. Although we were trying to plug Naji's bleeding, I remained concerned that we could be flanked and overrun by undetected insurgents.

However, the ongoing gunfire and RPG explosions must have woken the local police outpost and soon enough I saw the cavalry coming to the rescue and took a breath of relief as I saw two Afghan National Police (ANP) gun trucks rushing to our location. Although the situation was still unstable and dangerous, my mind paused the fight or flight condition long enough for me to chuckle inside because when the two trucks pulled up to our location it was a like a clown car. I couldn't believe how many officers got out of those vehicles, maybe twenty or so, who were now spraying the hillside with their shiny, new American issued M-16's.

The police commander, who spoke English, ran to our position and started asking me and Danny who we were and what was happening. As if things couldn't get worse, before I could provide a SITREP (situation report) a rocket streaked from the hillside and impacted near the front end of one of the ANP trucks with a deafening explosion, partially destroying the front end of the truck and wounding two Afghan police officers. Apparently we had missed a small group of concealed insurgents off to the left side of the contiguous trench line. This group now began firing their rifles while the group on the right side began increasing their hostile fire that was becoming more accurate.

"God Almighty what the hell is happening!" Danny yelled out.

Probably not the right time for this thought to enter in my head but it did, our premonition was right. I should have listened to Danny and stayed in bed like everyone in our team house was probably doing this very minute!

Some of our guards, as well as several police officers, ran to the wounded officers and pulled them out of the line of fire. Meanwhile the police commander furiously yelled out orders in Dari to the other ANP officers who ran to their other truck and retrieved four RPG launchers. The officers loaded the tubes and began continuously firing the rockets into both sides of the hillside as the rest of us poured on small arms fire. After eight rockets impacting the hillside, it pretty much ended the attack. The Taliban were known to be elusive, hit and run guerilla fighters, so as soon as they got a taste of the ANP rockets they broke contact and melted away into the hillside. Although the firing from the hilltop had fallen silent, our guys as well as the ANP officers were still firing their weapons. Danny ran to their positions waving his arms and yelling at them to cease fire and eventually they powered down and complied.

Once we established that it was really over, I ordered one of our Afghan guards to continue aiming his weapon at the hillside and cover us. Then I gave a set of binoculars to Sejun and instructed him to continually scan the hillside looking for any movement! Sejun informed me that he had used up all six PKM ammo belts and if he saw any movement he'd fire them up with AK-47.

I simultaneously instructed Thapa to get the other guards and sweep the battle space for empty mags and any equipment or personal items that may have been dropped, then to personally inspect the burnt out SUV and recover any salvageable equipment.

Thapa replied, "Yes sir!" and moved quickly to get things sorted out.

With great urgency I called out to Danny who was still in a combat state of mind scanning the hillside with his M4, "let's get the mining equipment quick shit into our truck." We both ran to the river's edge and gathered our equipment and moved it all into my SUV.

After a brief period of time, Thapa ran to us and reported, "Sirs, all equipment is accounted for except for a radio charger, a case of MRE's, two coolers and some personal items belonging to the guards which were all destroyed."

"Good job Thapa!" Danny replied.

Me and Danny gingerly carried the wounded Naji and set him into the middle bench seat of Danny's SUV. Before departing we walked over to check on the wounded Afghan police officers and to thank the commander for his assistance. The ANP commander was very friendly but requested our names along with the name of our company which he documented into his pocket notebook.

Although our experience and training prevented the team from panicking and making fatal decisions, the implications of suffering three wounded, destruction of our armored SUV and one Afghan police gun truck was not lost on us.

Danny blurted out, "good God Sal, wonder how we're going to explain this cluster?"

"Not sure but I think we are going to have to take the medicine on this one and it ain't gonna taste good, partner!"

Danny began rubbing his hand on his forehead and moving his jaw up and down.

"You OK?" I asked.

"My ears are still ringing and have an RPG sized headache."

"Listen, get the Go-Bag and down a handful of aspirin, we have a long bumpy ride back home and we need to remain alert for any possible ambush along the roadway."

"Alright" he said dejectedly.

We started walking to our individual SUV's and I stopped and turned toward Danny, "You know, you were right all along!" as I shook my head. "I got greedy, gotta start listening to you more often," as my face spread from a frown into a grin.

"Next time partner, next time!" Danny responded with an uncertain smile that was short-lived.

I slid behind the wheel of the first SUV as Thapa and two Afghan guards also piled in while Danny, Sejun, the wounded Naji and the other guard loaded into the other SUV. Danny radioed me, "My SUV is UP and ready to roll."

I radioed back, "Let's roll, cover your sectors and stay alert." We cranked up our SUV's, dropped our manual transmissions into gear and roared back toward the paved roadway for a bat-out-of-hell accelerated trip back to the team house. Even after driving a few miles down the road we could see a column of thick black smoke shooting up into the clear mountain sky emanating from the burnt out hulls of the two destroyed vehicles which greatly added to my foreboding feeling that there were bad consequences ahead for us.

None of us were in a communicative mood but about one hour into the drive back I radioed Danny, "how's Naji doing?"

Danny swiveled around and saw Naji with his now blood soaked combat dressings, "Naji, how you feeling?" Naji responded with a nod of the head and a thumbs-up. "Sal, he's conscious and seems to be stable. The sooner we get him into our clinic the better! "

I replied, "I'll contact the TOC and have the medic and his team standing by."

"Good call!, I'll let Naji know that Doc will probably give him a couple of happy pills that'll make him feel real good!" At hearing that Naji gave Danny a smile and another thumbs-up.

Two hours later, we entered the team house courtyard and saw that Obie, the team medic and his Afghan medic trainees were waiting in the parking lot.

Obie ran to Danny's vehicle, bent into the SUV and evaluated Naji's wounds. Obie assessed that Naji didn't appear to have bullet wounds and calculated that he was in stable condition. Obie ordered the Afghan medics to quickly but gently move the injured man to the team house clinic. As the Afghans were removing Naji out of the armored vehicle, Obie approached us and asked with an incredulous tone, "what the hell happened? Were you on a mission on a Friday?"

Danny responded, "Not really, we . ."

Obie, who was a former U.S. Army medic and longtime contractor took a look at the expression on our faces and he immediately perceived trouble, "oh shit, don't tell me anymore, I don't want get dragged into whatever mess this is!"

We asked Obie if Mike was around and he informed us that he was in Jalalabad and wouldn't return to our compound until late tonight and with that, Obie gave us one last glare of distress and briskly walked away toward the clinic.

8

P.N.G.'D AFGHANISTAN

Omnis cum in tenebris praesertim vita laboret.

[Life is one long struggle in the dark] – Lucretius

As we unpacked the gear, we looked inside Danny's SUV and saw the middle leather bench seat stained with blood. Danny turned toward me and said in a dispirited tone, "I feel a shit hitting the fan moment coming!"

"I'm afraid so partner but all is not lost! There'll be other opportunities." Without a word spoken, Danny shot me an are you crazy, puzzled look.

Unbeknownst to Danny, for months I had been planning another venture that was a lot closer to home, in México. In fact, during our eight months in Afghanistan I thought a lot and extensively planned unearthing a buried horde of gold in México.

An hour or so later we finished storing the gear and cleaning our weapons, Thapa caught us in the hallway and assured us that the SUV's would be washed and cleaned with not a hint of blood in the interior. We thanked him and asked him to tell the team they performed like professionals and we'd be supplying certificates of commendation to everyone.

"Hell, Sal, we better get to the clinic and check on Naji."

"Yeah, let's do it then finish the rest of what needs to be done before the shit storm begins!"

As we approached the clinic, as usual all the seats outside were occupied by some of our Afghan employees waiting to be seen for the daily this and that Afghanistan ailments, which usually consisted in asking for medicines for relatives. We peeked in the door and saw Obie and his Afghan medical trainees working on two Afghans laying on tables while Naji laid on the third table. Naji had an IV and monitors hooked up to him and clean bandages covering his wounds. "Hey Obie," I called out. "OK if we talk to Naji for a few seconds?"

"Yea but make it quick, we're busy in here right now."

Naji's had his face and arms washed and his bandages changed and looked a lot better. We approached Naji and Danny spoke first, "hey Naji, how you feeling?" He groggily raised his head with much effort and uttered something like hello boss.

"Did the Doc give you some happy medicine?" I asked.

He grinned and nodded his head. Naji was clearly out of it with pain meds so we shook hands with him and let Doc know if he needed anything we'd take care of it.

As we walked out we asked Obie about Naji's prognosis. Obie replied, "It's good, possibly a mild concussion, no imbedded bullets or shrapnel fragments, just lacerations to the face and arms, lost a bit of blood but he'll be up and running in a week or so. We'll stabilize and monitor him here for a day or two then send him home to rest."

We retreated to our rooms, removed our dirty, blood splattered BDU's and hoped to flush the filth and bad juju of the day down the drain. As much as we wanted to just lock ourselves in our rooms we still had to go downstairs to the TOC and complete and incident report and Use of Force form which would take hours.

We completed all the required documents in a few hours and put them in Mike's tray. We glanced at each other and without another word we retreated to our rooms to await the morning's wrath.

The next morning the two of us went up to the dining room in full exhaustion mode sporting blood shot eyes as sleep had been impossible with so much weighing on us. We dared not look for Mike so we finished eating and returned to our rooms not knowing what to expect. Maybe they would take into account all the good work we'd done but maybe not. At noon Mike got on his two way radio and ordered Thapa to locate me and Danny and bring us to his office.

Thapa knocked on our doors and he looked distressed so we knew the drill. Thapa walked us to Mike's office and as soon as we walked in he said, "Thapa, thanks, you can go back to your duties, please, close the door behind you!" Although we'd discussed being ready to take our medicine, once we saw Mike's grim look we knew things were worse than we imagined. "Have a seat," Mike said coldly.

"I was notified of the incident last night. I reviewed your reports as did our Embassy. The State Department then called me and I received a full briefing which included reports from ANP headquarters about your incident. Needless to say I was on the phone until 0200 hours, shortly thereafter I caught a chopper to Kabul to prepare for the shit storm that I knew was coming. I'm not even going to ask what the hell you two were doing in Baghlan Province on a Friday when everyone in the entire country is resting. No, I won't," as he paused and shook his head in anger, "what's done is done everything else is a moot point!"

"Mike as usual, me and Danny go out on Fridays to get some clean fresh air in the mountains and clear our heads, I realize it was a bad decision, I mean . ."

Mike abruptly shut me down, "Well let me tell you about your bad decision. This incident has stirred up a hornets nest here in Afghanistan, in Washington D.C. and our company's corporate office!" Looking down at papers scattered on his desk he continued, "let's see, one company armored vehicle with all its electronic equipment, completely destroyed to the tune of 300K, one Afghan Police gun truck destroyed, to the tune of 50K, one wounded company security guard and two wounded Afghan police officers, extensive collateral damage to homes in that mud village which the U.S. will have to pay compensation to the villagers and local officials and approximately five thousand rounds expended and thank God no civilian casualties!"

We shot glances at each other as our mouth twisted with a grim reverse smile that gave away our fear that a get ready to go to jail was oh-shit moment was imminent.

Mike continued, "Needless to say, last night I was chewed out by the State Department RSO then this morning caught hell during a conference call with several high level executives from our company. Everyone asked the same questions, why the hell were our security operators, on their day off, engaging in what they term offensive combat against a large Taliban force in Baghlan Province? Oh, by the way, that skirmish has caused an alert throughout the eastern part of the country requiring a hasty redeployment of Afghan military components!"

Me and Danny tried apologizing but realized it would be hopeless to say anything, explanations were beyond futile.

When Mike removed his glasses and shifted his eyes from the reports on his desk to us I knew our medicine was about to be doled out. "Bottom line men, State Department has forced my hand. I regret to inform you that you two are officially Persona Non Grata, P.N.G.'d from Afghanistan and you know what that means?"

"Yes we know," we said under our breath but also nodded in affirmation. We knew that term from the police captain but we never thought we'd hear it again.

It seemed like our winning ways would last   forever but in fact, our winning streak had abruptly come to an end. It was understood by all that we were living and working within the private military contractor world, no second chances, no suspensions, if you screw up, it was an aisle or window seat back to your home of record. Nevertheless, we were elated that we weren't in legal trouble for using deadly force and our punishment was nothing more than P.N.G.'d from Afghanistan!

In a clear and firm voice, Mike said, "boys, hands down, you are two of the best operators I've ever come across. Hate to lose you but folks with pay grades way above mine made their decision. Here you go," and handed each of us a large envelope. "Inside is your itinerary. You leave for the U.S. tomorrow at 0700 hours!"

We accepted the envelopes and looked at the contents. The itinerary was only two legs, Kabul to Dubai and then a straight shot to Dulles International Airport.

In a conciliatory manner I responded, "No worries Mike, we're truly sorry we caused you and the company so much trouble. You've been a great boss." We shook hands with Mike, got up and began walking out of his office when he called out to us.

"Hey you two one last thing, our compound is on lockdown by the Afghan government until you leave the country. Afghan forces will escort you to the airport tomorrow! Don't even think of leaving the team house for any reason, kapeesh?"

We answered in unison, "Yes sir!"

While doing the walk of shame back to our rooms to get our shit packed we paused to look at our seat assignments, "Finally some good news!" I exclaimed.

Oh yeah, what?"

"I got aisle seats all the way home!"

Danny looked at his tickets and immediately responded, "Are you shitting me? Middle seat all the way, ain't no way I can do that!"

With plans for the search of the buried horde in México pretty much set, I thought it best to get Danny in a good mood, "Don't sweat it partner, you can have my aisle seat on the fifteen hour flight from Dubai to Dulles."

"Er-well, OK, that's a deal," as Danny said with a wide grin.

Well, we were going home and although dejected at being fired and P.N.G'd from Afghanistan, we were excited about returning home. Once in our rooms we emailed our wives who were ecstatic that we were returning sooner than expected, safe and in one piece. We took the rest of the evening to write and print out letters of commendation for the guards involved in the gunbattle as well as letters of recommendations for all the Nepalese and Afghan guards on our contract. We never did get to sleep so by 0300 hours we were fully packed and ready to roll to the airport. The indefatigable Thapa as always saw to it that the chef was at his station to cook our breakfast at 0400 hours which allowed us to depart the compound by 0500 hours with a full stomach.

While everyone slept we had our breakfast, got our gear, looked at each other followed by a high-five and a declaration by me, "Our job is done here partner, let's get our asses home!"

"Thant's a big 10-4 partner, let's roll out of here," a reinvigorated Danny replied.

We walked out of the team house into the parking lot expecting to see one SUV staged with a driver. Instead we were startled to see our entire Nepalese and Afghan security team in formation wearing clean and pressed uniforms, standing in a parade rest formation. Incredibly stirring was that skinny-ass Naji was in the front of the formation with an IV sticking out of his arm, propped up by two of our Afghan medic trainees. Thapa saw us and called out in a booming authoritative voice, "Attenhuh!" The men smartly snapped to attention. "Sirs, the men would like you to inspect the team one last time."

We looked at each other and nodded as Danny replied, "we would be honored to do so Mr. Thapa."

I whispered to Thapa, "The letters of commendation are in your tray."

"Thank you so much sirs, the men will be very happy with those documents," he replied effusively!

With that said, we walked up to Thapa and Sejun who was standing next to Thapa and saluted the two men. Thapa and Sejun gave us crispy salutes in return. We proceeded to walk up and down the line and salute and thank the Afghan security guards and we both gave Naji a hug and a job well done thank you.

When we finished, Thapa said to us, "thank you sirs, it's been an honor serving under your command. I'm very, very sad you two leaving us!" Thapa and Sejun gave us hugs and we shook hands in a final farewell.

During our hundreds of missions we had built a strong bond with the Nepalese Gurkhas as well as with our Afghan security team members. However, the Nepalese stood apart, their discipline and unparalleled loyalty was beyond anything me and Danny had ever experienced.

We felt fortunate to have had the opportunity to work alongside these fearless, hardworking security operators.

We put all our gear in the truck and as we were preparing to mount up we heard someone calling out to us from the building. "Hey, you two!" We turned around and saw it was Mike standing by the front door of the team house. "Take care you two maniacs!" He yelled out with a big smile on his face. He saluted us and we returned the salute in respect for our former boss!

As we drove out the gates Danny looked around and said, "We don't have weapons, sure hope it'll be a safer ride to the airport this time around."

"We'll be fine, our bad juju is behind us now!"

As we pulled out of the compound there was a massive Afghan military and police presence waiting for us. Four Afghan police trucks pulled in front of us as they led the convoy with a shit load of Afghan military Humvees behind us. "Damn, I feel like a head of state with that kind of escort."

"Let's hope they take us to the airport and not to the dreaded Pul-e-Charkhi Prison," Danny said in a hushed tone. Pul-e-Charkhi was a horrific place where westerners were typically detained for all types of crimes and shenanigans.

Thankfully the ride to the airport went without any shots fired or other related drama. At the airport parking lot we quickly un-assed our gear and started walking to the terminal. Some of the Afghan police and military personnel were grinning and waived to us. We didn't know if they were thinking good riddance of these crazy Americans or maybe they were supportive that we fought alongside them in a battle against the Taliban, I guess we'll never know what was on their mind.

We went through the Kabul Airport security screening kabuki show characterized by airport security personnel putting on a big show with little gained as they searched for contraband but really looking for items to pilfer from westerners. We waited at our departure gate with great anticipation, nervously rubbing our hands hoping that a suicide bomber attack at the airport, a common occurrence, would at least wait until we were up and away into the clouds.

Well, boarding time came and now it was time to get mentally prepared for the Kabul Airport boarding challenge. As usual, airport unofficial officials standing around doing nothing, passengers refusing to obey the boarding by zone announcements resulting in multiple boarding lines with hordes pushing and jockeying to board. After twenty-minutes or so we finally got in our seats soaking wet from the hot terminal and onboarding WWE wrestling match. The moment came and soon enough we were wheels up on our 737-200 as we said goodbye to Afghanistan!

9

BACK HOME, REGOUPING, PLOTTING

Nil satis nisi optimum. [Nothing but the best is good enough] – Unknown

December 2003

Without Danny's knowledge, before departing Afghanistan, I purchased two VIP lounge passes through the internet in preparation for our eight hour layover at the Dubai Airport. I figured we could use the rest and would put Danny in a more receptive mood for joining my next treasure scheme.

After three hours of bouncing up and down as we flew through the mountain ranges we finally arrived at the Dubai Airport, terminal two. We transited to terminal one and checked into the VIP lounge. We'd been up now for nearly thirty hours without sleep and were weary with the thought of the brutally long flight ahead of us to the Washington, D.C. area.

The VIP lounge was a blessing. We were able to shower, eat pretty damn good food and kick back in comfortable leather seats far away from the hordes of travelers transiting through Dubai.

Although we were paid a hefty salary during our eight months on the Afghanistan contract along with the gold ore and gems we shipped home, it was far from what we needed to make a significant difference in our lives! With that thought in mind and noticing that Danny was relaxed, I began the arduous task of convincing him to step out of his comfort zone once again.

"Hey Danny, did I ever tell you about this incredible story I stumbled on many years ago while I was assigned to the detective bureau?"

"Which one, you've recounted so much BS over the past twenty-five years that . . ."

"Nah, this one is gold," I said in a hushed tone making sure no one was eavesdropping. "I got this information from no less than Doctor Benitez, remember him?"

Pausing for a few seconds, "Yeah, I vaguely remember you talking about Doc Benitez years ago, the cardiologist, right?" as he shrugged his shoulders with disinterest.

"Yeah that's the one. I got to know the doc after his house was burglarized. I worked the case and resolved it within one week with two arrests. I recovered every single item stolen from his home. After the case was adjudicated in court, I transported all the stolen items back to his home. We talked for hours and I recounted some of my metal detecting stories and search for treasure. Out of nowhere he springs this wild tale on me that had been kept quietly in his family for nearly a century."

"OK, tell me, what's the secret he sprung on you?"

"This is what he told me, the Hidalgo family were multi-generational wealthy landowners who owned a ten thousand acre cattle and sheep ranch along with a huge agricultural operation in northern México. The family did most of their livestock sales across the border in the U.S. but because banking facilities in that part of México were operated by bankers of dubious integrity, they transferred much of their banknotes to a bank in Texas. However, over a period of forty years, many transactions resulted in the accumulation of a huge horde of Mexican and American gold coins. The family periodically transported crates of the coins to a central bank in México City. This procedure came to an abrupt halt after banditos waylaid a group of armed couriers transporting a gold shipment to the capital. The couriers were murdered and the bandits got away with four boxes filled with mostly gold coins.

Thereafter the family settled on stashing the coins in their Hacienda, using it for payroll and other expenses. Overtime they accumulated many crates filled with gold coins more than they ever needed to pay expenses."

"Why are you telling me this lore of the old wests B.S. story Sal?"

"No, no, just hear me out brother! When the parents died in the late 1800's the two brothers continued running this money making enterprise and were too busy to do anything with the crates of coins stored in the Hacienda. You still with me?"

"Yeah, I'm just taking it all in."

"OK, don't fall asleep on me!"

"Aha!"

"Alright, so now let's fast forward to México in the early 1900's. A peasant led revolution erupts in many parts of the country led by the likes of Pancho Villa and Emiliano Zapata. These two and their posse's began tear-assing and rampaging throughout México and confiscating large tracts of wealthy landowner's property. Well, sometime in 1914, the two elderly Hidalgo brothers, who had no other living family members, became so concerned about their safety that they abandoned their Hacienda and fled to the United States and never returned to México. But, here's the bombshell, before the brothers fled they had Franciscan monks help them bury the boxes of gold coins approximately ten paces west of a great five-hundred year old Socorro Oak tree which was located near the church. This tree is said to be the size of a building!"

"What the hey, a church, how'd that get into the story?"

"Doc Benitez told me the Hidalgo family was a religious family, so much so that in the mid 1800's they constructed a church on their estate. They named the church, la Iglesia del los Santos which translates to the Church of Saints."

"Sure Sal but C'mon, even if this story is true I'm sure the monks or someone associated with the order came back and recovered the boxes!"

"Yeah I thought about that too but when you separate the chaff from the wheat, the facts point conclusively that the gold coins remain buried and untouched since the day they were interned."

"How do you figure that?"

"Because over many years the family contributed substantially to the Franciscan order that had a strong presence in México. The monks conducted weekly services in the Hacienda church for family members, business associates, elected officials and even special worship services for Hacienda employees. So when the time came for the brothers to ask the Friars for assistance, they complied and buried the boxes. These monks cultivated a life of poverty and sacrifice so when the Hidalgo brother requested their assistance Friars quickly and quietly buried the crates, probably never knowing or caring what the contents were. And by all accounts, the two brothers lived and died in the U.S. never setting foot in México again!"

I could almost see the wheels turning inside Danny's head and the sound of a bill counting machine spinning hundred dollar bills, so when he asked, "So how does Doc Benitez fit in into this story?" I knew I had definitely piqued his interest.

"Doc told me it was a touchy subject for the family. You see Doc's Mexican Great Grandfather had dual citizenship with the U.S. and was very wealthy in his own right and well connected with American politicians. With the Mexican revolution in full swing, Doc's relative assisted the Hidalgo brothers rush the transfer of large sums of money into their bank in Texas. If I understood Doc Benitez correctly, some of the funds from this account found its way into the pockets of key American officials if you get my drift, which allowed the two brothers to obtain expedited entry into the U.S. when the time was right. Since Doc's great grandfather was wealthy in his own right he had no interest in digging up the boxes. Now, eighty-eight years later this event became nothing more than a tale within the Benitez family who were always wealthy so no one in their family ever gave a shit about those boxes! That is until me and you came along," I quipped with a big smile!

"So that's it, we had a shitload of deadly encounters in Afghanistan, we get P.N.G.'d from Afghanistan and now you want me to head off to México and search for that fairy tale treasure?"

"Yeah, that's right, pretty much, yeah."

"Hold on, let me check my calendar, yep it's Friday, sorry but I have a No on Friday policy, ask me in a year or so," Danny said as he crossed his arms and frowned in disbelief.

"'Look Danny, I've been planning the recovery of these boxes for the past several months. The boxes are buried just over the U.S. México border so it would be an in and out, quick shit operation! OK, so we had a bit of a hiccup in Afghanistan but my plan did get us beaucoup money, no?"

"Yes it did and that's enough for me! We almost got ourselves and others killed plus we got expelled from a country," raising his voice "you hear me, expelled!"

"So what, we were expelled from Afghanistan, who cares? We weren't planning on vacationing there any time soon," I emphasized.

"I've been crunching your numbers Danny and . ."

"The hell you mean, crunching my numbers, you're my accountant now?"

I chuckled and replied, "Look partner, you and me are in the same boat! We've got big dreams with bills out the Yazoo! Tell me if I'm wrong, your two girls are getting ready to attend an out of state Ivy League college, you got a mortgage, credit card bills and then there's that RV you've been dreaming of for decades. If my police math is correct you'll need about a cool million to make your dreams come true and still have a buck, three-fifty walking around pocket change, now did I get anything wrong?"

"So, let me see if I have a clear understanding of your proposal, we're going to stroll south of the border for a few days then return home with a million dollars, just like that, ay?"

"No partner, you've got that wrong, you left out the S at the end of the word million!"

Danny's face now showed that he was seriously mulling over what he just heard then turned away in deep reflection.

I paused for a few minutes to let the information sink in, then after a heavily thoughtful sigh Danny blurted out, "Let's say we find the crates, how the hell do we get them across the border?"

Exuding confidence I replied, "We don't have to take anything across the border no matter how many crates we unearth!"

"Can't wait to hear you how you're going to make that possible?"

Once we find the crates and dig them out we'll transport them to a secure storage facility near the city of Hermosillo where no one asks questions. Once a month we'll fly directly from the U.S. to Hermosillo, rent a truck at the airport and transport a few crates to a metals dealer who's located a mere one hour drive from this storage facility."

"You telling me you're going to trust a Mexican metals dealer with millions in gold?"

"Get this, the dealer Enriquez, or Ernie which is what likes to be called, is Mex but he's a former U.S. Marine, of all things, so right away I had a bond with him. Me and Ernie have been going back and forth on emails for almost a year and we've got a solid agreement in place. He has a thriving pawn shop-scrap metals operation and he guarantees that not only can sell large volumes of gold coins but also has the ability to wire the proceeds to our LLC accounts in the U.S. So as a test run we'll inventory the contents of one box and transport it to his location then see if he can do what he says he can do!"

g"And what's Ernie's take on all the transactions?"

"He's agreed to a five percent fee of every transaction, no questions asked. So, if there's only five hundred gold coins in the twenty-five crates, at the current spot price of gold, the haul would amount to about twelve million dollars, my guy gets about $600K or so and he's super happy! Me and you walk away with about 11 million and we're very happy, too!"

"I have to admit it sounds plausible, if true, I mean all the pieces of the puzzle seem to be in place and you've got the recovery planned out pretty well, but . ."

"But, but, I can hear it in your voice, what? Did I miss something?"

"No, you haven't missed anything, I'm just thinking, we haven't even boarded the plane to get home. We haven't even set foot in the U.S. and here we are talking about leaving home again. How about spending some time with our family and enjoying the money we've made?"

"Look brother, me and you have literally sweated blood for twenty five years protecting the public at large, what do we have to show for it? Not enough, if you ask me! I'm not going to live the rest of my life like a regular Joe schmuck, not after everything we've been through!" I stressed.

"Can't argue with that," Danny said in agreement.

Now that I had infected Danny with a bad case of treasure fever it was time to close the deal. "I want you to think about those numbers. If the crates are exactly how they were described, then we split about eleven million! If there's more, then all the better, either way it's a win-win for everyone involved. For one thing you and Becky buy that RV you've been dreaming about and won't have to stress about a loan for the kid's college tuition. So how about it partner, we gonna keep our dream alive," I asked?

I'd been so absorbed recounting the Hidalgo brothers story that I lost track of time. The loud speaker in the lounge announced that our flight was ready for boarding so we had to scramble before I got a firm commitment from Danny.

We picked up our backpacks and departed the subdued stillness and fresh air environment of the VIP lounge and return to the heat and chaos of the boarding gate. In Kabul we were boarding about one hundred-thirty passengers. Now we were preparing to board a 747 with nearly four hundred passengers. The boarding this time was a bit more organized but passengers still cut in line, pushed and shoved to get ahead of the next person. We finally battled our way on board with our shirts drenched in sweat but energized that this was our final leg on the way home.

As promised, I gave up my aisle seat to Danny and pretty much left him to his thoughts to mull over the rich possibilities that awaited us in Mexico if he dared to seize opportunity. The only time I really bothered Danny was during the evening dinner meal service where I planted one last thought for him to think about during the long, extremely uncomfortable flight.

"Danny, have you ever heard some of the quotes from Seneca?"

Danny shrugged his shoulders and said, "No idea, was he an Indian Chief or something, he replied as he kept on eating?

"No man, he was a philosopher from Spain, man, you've got to get past the sports pages! Anyway, one of his famous quotes says something like, 'A man who craves more, is poor.' Well, I call bullshit on that! I want more, I don't want to settle for a comfortable middle class life. I want to be freed from penny pinching and be able to think about big picture issues as opposed to worrying about where am I going to find the money to put a new roof on my house."

Danny nodded pensively at what I had just said then he finished his meal and fell into a deep sleep for most of the remaining flight. We landed at Dulles International Airport exhausted but in good spirits. We were anticipating seeing our wives and children for the first time in nearly nine months and spending a peaceful Christmas holiday with them.

It wasn't until we started walking to the baggage area that the enormity of the past eight months began hitting us. "Man we're home," I exclaimed loudly with a clenched fist in the air!

"We made it Sal! Damn it's good to be back home," Danny said as we bantered back and forth and enjoyed breathing in the freedom filled air of America.

We anxiously waited for our gear at the carousel then briskly walked out to the lobby area looking for our families.

And there they were, our wives and children waiting for us with open arms. We got hugs and some tears shed by Jean and Becky knowing we were home safe. While walking to the parking lot area I approached Danny and asked him to walk with me for a second. We left the wives cheerfully chatting and walking behind us.

"Hey Danny, I got to know if you're on board for the south of the border excursion."

"Why don't you give me about six months to think about it."

"Alright fair is fair, have it your way, we'll let lucky lady Saint-Gaudens decide this again, 50-50! If you get it right I'll walk away and we'll wait till the summer before I ask you again. If lady luck falls on my side, we'll leave March 1."

"No way Sal, put that damn coin away," he warned with a worried look on his face.

"Here it goes, call it, call it Danny!"

"I'm leaving," Danny started walking away and then quickly turned while my lucky coin was still in the air and thundered, "Heads!"

10

MÉXICO

*Danger, if you meet it promptly and without flinching you
will reduce the danger by half. Never run away from
anything. Never!   Winston Churchill*

I t was tails again!

Sometimes I wish I was less ambitious and less
adventuress like normal people but I just don't know
how to be anything else.

So when I broached the subject of the buried crates
in México with Jean she almost laughed as if I were joking!
However she quickly realized I was serious and she shook
her head and said, "Alright, tell me about this gold," as she
rolled her eyes waiting to hear the sordid details.

I told her the same Hidalgo Brothers story that I had
recounted to Danny. She was skeptical but didn't draw
the line in the sand and say no. From the start of our lives
together, she knew that I was a restless soul and a bit of a
swashbuckler. I'd served in the Corp, worked as a private

security guard in Rhodesia and if I hadn't been called up for a job with the police department in 1978, I would have been off to France for a five year hitch in the French Foreign Legion. So after a few tense days she came around , like always, reiterated "take care of yourself and for God's sake keep an eye on Danny!"

However, at the Mahoney household it was a completely different story! Explaining Afghanistan was difficult but explaining Mexico was definitely a tough sell for Danny.

"Really Danny, you just got home. It's too far, it's too dangerous and it's too soon for you to be even thinking about taking off with crazy Sal again on another one of his get rich quick schemes," Becky said emphatically!

"Look hon, we'll be just over the Arizona-México border. It's a get in, get out trip and I think the prospects for a big score is better than a fifty-fifty proposition!"

"So, you're going to follow up surviving an attack by the Taliban in Afghanistan by rushing off to Mexico and tangle with drug gangs. It's a sure path to the morgue Danny, it's absurd for you to even be contemplating it!"

This back and forth went on for weeks but Becky eventually relented, especially after numerous phone calls and meet-ups with Jean.

Finally, the big Irishman was onboard but of course with a permission slip from his boss to go hunting for treasure one more time. I had my wingman now which was going to be critical in not only recovering the gold but also staying alive during the search.

I knew research on this outing was critical because I had a hunch that we needed to be prepared for the unexpected! I scoured the internet for information on the Hidalgo brothers then went to the Library of Congress but came up with a big fat zero. I was getting a bit worried that those two dudes never really existed and I was chasing an old treasure legend!

Another problem I encountered was obtaining reliable information regarding security issues in Soccoro México. Before we got boots on the ground we certainly needed a clear understanding of the dangers we may encounter and prepare for.

I decided it was time to take a different approach to gathering the Intel. I started calling around my Marine Corps network and sure enough through a friend of a friend of friend, I made a connection with a U.S. Department of State, special agent (RSO) who was assigned to the U.S. Consulate in Matamoros, México. I phoned RSO **James C.** but he let me know that he could not brief me on security matters over the phone. He agreed to meet with me at the consulate, so I made arrangements to travel to the consulate and find out what me and Danny might be facing in Soccoro.

I hated spending money to travel to México for what would probably amount to no more than a one hour conversation that may or may not be of any use. Add to that my apprehension of going at it alone on this first leg but the vision of those twenty-five crates was sufficient inducement for me to push on. I didn't want to get Danny involved in the boring, often tedious part of the planning plus I thought it best to let him cool his heels at home since our experience in Afghanistan was still fresh in our heads. The day came, Jean drove me to Dulles Airport and although she was a bit concerned about me travelling solo to México she knew it was an in and out fact finding trip.

Jean dropped me off curbside and from there I flew to the Brownsville International Airport in Texas. The Brownsville Airport was a tiny thing but very convenient for getting in and out quickly. I took a taxi and the three mile ride to the U.S. Consulate in Matamoros, Mexico took almost forty-five minutes due to heavy traffic and people walking in the streets which added to the insane gridlock. The town of Matamoros looked sketchy with vendors everywhere selling trinkets and large groups of men hanging around looking suspicious. There were huge crowds in front of the consulate and a line that snaked around the block. I approached a security guard standing outside the consulate and asked him to point me in the right direction since I had an appointment with RSO James C. The guard escorted me past the crowds and into a hallway that had an arched, bullet resistant barrier window with a talk through port. I slipped my passport through a slide tray and informed the lady I had an appointment with the RSO. The window was like the Get Smart TV show with that fakakta 'cone of silence,' she couldn't hear me and I couldn't hear her but eventually I think she understood me because she picked up her phone and motioned for me to wait while she talked to someone.

A few minutes later a man in a suit came out and introduced himself as Assistant RSO James C. I introduced myself and we shook hands. I followed him to his office and he began asking questions with a focus on what exactly we were coming to México for. I was as honest as possible and informed him, "Me and my partner are going to do a little prospecting in the Sonora desert area."

He shook his head and gave me a serious look, as if implying that I must be out of my mind. RSO James C. went into his security briefing, rattling off the names of the different cartels and the regions they control, pointing to color coded pins on a wall map. He went on to say that the situation had become increasingly deadly for everyone because the conflict between government forces and the cartels as well as the intra-cartel violence had spilled over into the innocent civilian population. The result being thousands of civilians being killed simply for being in the wrong place at the wrong time.

RSO James C. highlighted the fact that there were two cartels currently fighting aggressively for the Soccoro area territory along the U.S. México border. His briefing went on to say that the Soccoro area was now considered a hotspot with a reputation as one of the most violent cartel areas in México. Yikes, I gulped hard, this war zone was exactly where the two of us would be searching for the treasure.

After the briefing I asked him if he could assist us in obtaining expedited Mexican weapons carry permits. He looked at me for a few seconds with a puzzled expression then just busted out laughing. He informed me that there was no such thing and that possession of guns and even knives by foreigners was strictly forbidden and strictly enforced. In fact, even U.S. Federal agents coming to México on official business had to leave their weapons in the U.S.

I winced at that unexpected news, a real blow to my confidence. How the hell were we supposed to protect ourselves in one of the most dangerous areas of México.

At the conclusion of our meeting RSO James C. left me with two options. He proffered, "First, don't go, but if you do decide to proceed with your plans, get in and out as quickly as possible. If you linger around too long you'll attract too much attention, greatly increasing the odds of you guys getting kidnapped and winding up with your heads cut off!"

He provided emergency contacts for the consulate but warned that Sonora was too far from the consulate to provide any immediate assistance should an emergency occur. He provided Mexican law enforcement contacts but warned they were not reliable and may not have an English speaker to assist you in an emergency.

With a look of trepidation, RSO James C. said that as one former Marine to another, think about the dangers I would face should I decide to move forward with my project. With that last thought he wished me luck and escorted me out of the consulate. Due to the insecurity around the consulate, the RSO took the initiative to have a staff member arrange to have a taxi standing by for me. As soon I exited the consulate I saw the taxi waiting for me but I had to turn around and take one last look at this small building with a huge American flag waving on the roof, a huge wave of patriotism and gratitude came over me, America standing tall all around the world.

On the taxi ride to the border crossing in route to the Brownsville Airport, I was deep in thought and racked my brain on how I was going to explain the situation to Danny. There was no way to sugar coat what we were facing. No way was I going to withhold or underestimate the extent of the danger, he had to know the truth and I'd let the chips fall where they may! I think both of us would be willing to deal with the danger but our inability to be armed was a huge hurdle and one that I was sure Danny would pepper me with 'what if' questions to no end!

I arrived at the airport without any issues and had four hours to kill before my flight departed. I took the opportunity to purchase twenty-two thousand pesos at a cost of two thousand dollars and planned on giving half to Danny for expenses or situations where a bribe was warranted for information or just to stay alive!

It was an uneventful flight back to the Washington, D.C., Jean was at the airport waiting to pick me up without any parking issues. We were on the road back home and in less than five minutes she asked, "OK, what's wrong?" Jean was always perceptive at reading my body language.

I replied, "No problems, everything went well. It's just that . .," I paused for a second not wanting to alarm her, "ah, well, we're not going to be able to carry weapons in México."

"So you're going to scrap the project I hope?"

"Not yet, it's not a deal killer. I just have to put pencil to paper and come up with a solution to overcome these obstacles."

"Hun, you barely got out of Afghanistan with your skin. You sure about this, we really don't need the money."

I took in a deep breath to ask her outright. If she said no, I would accept her decision and call it off, "Hon, are you OK with it if I decide to go?"

"Sal, we've been together for nearly thirty years. I trust your judgement and your perseverance, if this is something you have to do, then I'm OK with you trying to find those crates, what could go wrong, right?"

That got a laugh out of me but I was sure glad that Becky was onboard with my plans. She was right, what could go wrong, probably a boatload could I thought to myself!

Well, we now had our wives consent to find those crates full of life altering riches but waltzing south of the border and unearthing those crates was definitely shaping up to be a tough nut to crack. I was well aware that danger comes in different packages but I wasn't expecting that the danger package for México would be riskier than Afghanistan on oh so many levels.

In Afghanistan we were earning a damn good salary plus I had the GPS coordinates for a starting point for locating the gold and gems plus we had our own heavily armed tactical team. This time around we had no exact location, no weapons and there was no cavalry coming to our rescue! Regardless of the inherent dangers, I was committed to uncovering the truth whether or not the Hidalgo brothers treasure story was real or just another treasure legend!

Over the next few weeks I met with Danny several times and at first he was shocked not only at the insecurity in Soccoro but also the fact that we would be unable to carry weapons in such a lawless area. Relying on RSO James C.'s advice we came to a consensus that this would be the first of many in-out quick trips to the Soccoro region. The goals on this first trip were to locate the Hidalgo Hacienda, then confirm the existence of the church and find the five-hundred year old massive tree. Time permitting, we'd scan the area with our metal detector and confirm the crates were still there. If all our goals were met then we'd return home and plan for the next phase.

During our last meeting, I gave Danny eleven thousand pesos for expenses in which he responded with, "What's this, a bribe?"

"Ha ha no brother it's a loan, you see each gold coin in those crates is worth about one thousand dollars, so when we divvy up the loot, I get one extra coin," I replied.

"Hell," he said laughing, "if we find those crates I'll give you two coins!"

"Deal," I replied.

Well, March rolled around and it was time for me and Danny to leave home again. In the interim I got my first taste of full retirement. After spending the last few months at home with no pressures and no one telling me where to go and what to do, except for Becky that is, hell yes I could get used to that!

This time we drove to the airport in separate cars to give us some private time with our wives. We got dropped off at the departure terminal and we met up at our gate. With the long flights to and from Afghanistan in mind, my back, knees and ass were already aching at the thought of once again flying shitty economy class out of Dulles Airport. We agreed beforehand to buy seats next to each other which would give us time to go over the plan and tie up any loose ends.

Danny had the aisle seat and I was stuck in the middle seat. I hate flying and get bored within no time flat. I made an English Spanish cheat sheet and the flight to México was a good time to keep practicing some useful phrases. As I read in my best Spanglish, "En donde esta Iglesia del los Santos?"

Danny turned his head and muttered under his breath, "What the hell did I get into this time."

I ignored Danny's protestations and continued, "Por favor, me puede ayudar?" Danny put on his noise cancelling headphones and ignored my Spanglish.

We arrived at the Tucson International Airport after our two stop flights turned into an eight hour journey. We hustled to the car rental counter and began the process of renting a pickup truck we had reserved. The rental agent was helpful since we didn't know squat about driving into México. "Here's your rental papers for your truck along with México rental insurance. Don't forget to stop when you enter México at the immigration office and get your papers squared away, especially the vehicle import ticket so you can legally drive past the twenty-five mile tourist checkpoint, any questions?"

I replied, "No sir, looks like everything's in order. Thank you very much for your assistance." As we walked away I noticed the agent gave us the same look as the two guys we replaced in Afghanistan. A look that said, these two gringos are never going to be seen again!

We started the long meandering drive to the city of Douglas, Arizona, the last town in America before entering México. The two hour drive was relatively smooth but it was getting late and we wanted to get to our hotel in Soccoro before dark. We finally made it to the border and saw the Green overhead sign ENTERING MÉXICO. I yelled, out, "It's time for some disorder on the border!"

Danny immediately responded, "Oh crap, I've got a bad feeling about this," as we pushed on and crossed into México.

I snickered and deflected Danny's trepidation, "Millions of Americans come to México to vacation! Think of this trip as a vacation where we get paid millions just for stopping by and saying Hola Amigos!"

Upon crossing the border we stopped at the Mexican Immigration Office and squared away our paperwork for visas and vehicle permit. As we left the immigration office and got into our truck and uttered out loud, "How about we dig up those crates and get our eleven million dollars partner on this first trip!"

Danny replied, "Right on brother, no drama this time around OK!"

"You got it" which was followed by our customary high-five!

I continued driving while Danny studied the road map using a small flashlight to illuminate the pages. "Looks like a straight shot down México highway 17. The Hotel Duerma Bien [*Hotel Sleep Well*] should be on the left side," Danny advised.

"Copy, I'm sure it'll be a half star hotel," I quipped sarcastically!

We easily dodged the occasional potholes along the highway while the sun still provided a bit of light before sunset but now darkness was all around us. The road seemed to melt into the night causing us to drive at a snail's pace. We gingerly rambled down the desolate two lane highway for nearly two hours and occasionally came across semi-trucks but very few passenger cars, this whole area seemed like the far edge of the world. We finally saw the sign for our hotel and it was comforting since we were ready for a hot meal and a good night's sleep. As we pulled into the parking lot we saw the motel was shabby looking, as if it had been shut down years ago. The single-story motel was a long L-shaped structure with rooms opening directly onto a parking lot, making it easy to unload gear from our truck. Danny looked in disbelief, "Damn, this isn't even a half star hotel, how many days we here for?"

Yeah it was a shithole but I secured rooms in this hotel because it was in the outskirts of the city. I took RSO James C.'s advice to heart, keep a low profile and don't linger too long. There were better hotels in town but the Duerma Bien would keep us away from too many eyes!

We walked inside to what appeared to be a restaurant that also functioned as the front desk-registration office. The place had a distinct unpleasant musty smell that reminded me of abandoned buildings that drug users used as a crack house. We approached the man behind the registration desk who was a rotund man in his forties, wearing a dirty white shirt and hair greased back. "Good evening," I said to see if he understood English.

In good enough English he replied, "Bienvenidos Señores, you must be Señor Rossi and Señor Mahooney."

I looked at Danny with a smile and responded, "Yes, Rossi and Mahooney," as I looked on a frowning Danny.

"Señor, we want two rooms, side by side in the quietest part of this hotel," I asserted.

"Si, no problem, we take good care of you here," replied the clerk. "After you put your luggage away please come to the dining room, Carmelita will get our chef to prepare a good hot meal for you."

"OK, gracias." replied Danny.

"OK now, here are your keys. My name is Carlos the hotel manager, let me know if you boys need anything, maybe ladies for a party, si," as he flashed a big grin.

I sternly told the clerk, "No, gracias," as me and Danny flashed a hardened glare at him. I'm sure he got the message because he never again offered us anything other than food and asking if everything was OK with our rooms.

We stepped outside and noticed a man in what passed for a uniformed security guard patrolling the parking lot. We approached him and confirmed he worked for the motel and that there was a guard on duty around the clock. The security guard spoke English well enough for us to arrange for special security. We offered the day and night shift guards ten dollars each, per day, for safeguarding our rooms during the day and our truck during the night. The security guard was ecstatic at the offer and was more than happy to earn the extra money.

With that arrangement in place we got back in the truck and drove to the two rooms at the end of property. Luckily the clerk had put us in rooms furthest away from the restaurant area which is where we saw what looked like working ladies walking in and out of several rooms. I turned to Danny and said, "Hey, the people here are real sketchy. I think it's best not to ask anybody here for information of the church or the Hidalgo brothers."

"Sure thing. I was also tracking in that direction, the fewer people that know our business, the better!"

We stepped into our rooms to check them out and I quickly noticed the stained carpeting and plaster peeling off the walls. "Oh man, what a shithole, home sweet home," I muttered to myself. We made a couple of trips back and forth from the rooms to the truck and finally got all our gear stowed away.

Danny being the eating machine that he is called out, "Hey, let's get some food, I'm starving."

"Roger that," as I suddenly remembered being hungry myself.

We left the truck in front of the rooms and the security guard who was nearby gave us a thumbs-up. Although it was only 9:30 PM, the dining room was empty and Danny, who was starving, cried out, "shit, is the kitchen closed?" They must have heard us because immediately a middle aged woman scrambled out of the kitchen and seated us. The lady had the complexion of an old penny, wearing a somewhat dirty but brightly colored flowery traditional Mexican dress. We wondered what language she would use so when she said, "buenas noches caballeros, mi nombre es Carmelita qué te gustaría comer?"

We realized ordering would consist of pointing at what we wanted on the menu which had photos of the actual meals. We played it safe and ordered chicken with refried beans and yellow rice and a couple of ice cold Dos Equis cervezas. While waiting for the food we shot the shit about the virtues of the hotel. "Hey, do the towels in your room look like they've been used to dry cars at a car wash," Danny asked sarcastically?

I replied, "No, not really, my towels looked like they were used to wipe the floor of a murder scene." We laughed followed by a high-five! We were pleasantly surprised by chef's well cooked and delicious meal. After that we immediately fast walked to our rooms for some much needed rest.

When I finally went to bed, I looked at the night stand box clock, it was 11 PM and as soon as my head hit the pillows, a tsunami wave of sleep engulfed me. The next conscious thing I remember was the sunlight pouring from the window shades that were pocked with large round holes which brought me back from the dead. I couldn't believe it was 0800 hours, as a very early riser, this was an aberration, hopefully Danny wouldn't be pissed.

I washed up and raced to the restaurant to get my breakfast. Not surprisingly, Danny had already demolished a six egg omelet, half a loaf of bread and was working on his fifth cup of coffee. I was super anxious to start looking for the Hidalgo Hacienda, so I wolfed down my breakfast and we took off on what I hoped would be a quick and profitable day.

11

GOLD FEVER

It's said that in search for treasure, a man can endlessly research, suffer, toil, starve and waste his life at the end of a shovel yet it won't bring gold a dammed inch closer to the surface!

Unknown

Day 1

We decided that until we located the Hidalgo property we would leave the metal detector and our surplus military folding shovels in our rooms and hoped the motel security guards would safeguard our equipment. We took off enthusiastically hoping that we'd find everything exactly the way it was described by Doc Benitez.

As we drove toward the town center it became evident that Soccoro, which was a mere two and one half hours from the U.S., was a crossroad for a lot of heavy trucking back and forth from the border.

The deeper we thrust into Soccoro, it became obvious that it was a town that time had passed by. The combination of pollution and dusty desert air made the visibility in mid-morning difficult. The walls on the buildings in the city center had black soot splotched top to bottom and an unhealthy smell of raw sewage permeated the air.

Once we found the town square we decided it was time to get out of our truck and begin our recon of the area and look for a central library. As we walked about it became evident that this town was not a tourist destination. We seemed to be the only foreigners so I turned toward Danny and asked him if he was getting the same vibes. "We're getting a lot of stares from the folks, ay?"

"Yeah, I don't like this. We're sticking out like T-bone steaks in a vegan restaurant."

We walked across the square, shuffled in and out of the stores and eventually found the town library, which turned out to be surprisingly well stocked with huge amounts of shelf space filled with a vast number of books, magazines and periodicals. However we discovered that all printed material was in Spanish. We approached an employee and asked her if she spoke English. The woman smiled and replied, "Un momento, conseguiré que alguien te ayude." Which I understood as, stand by while I get someone to assist you.

Sure enough, she returned with a well-dressed, college professor looking man who introduced himself in English, "Hello gentlemen, my name is Mister Serrano. I am the head librarian, how may I assist you?" We then exchanged pleasantries and introduced ourselves. Then we got down to brass tacks.

I informed Mr. Serrano of the reason for our visit, "Sir we are looking for the location of a church by the name of the Iglesia de los Santos."

Mr. Serrano got a confused look on his face and responded, "I know all the churches in our town and we have no such church. Are you sure you're in the correct town?"

We looked at each other as our hearts sank. I then interjected, "Mr. Serrano, this church was located on the Hidalgo brother's hacienda and we believe these men fled México for the United States sometime in 1914."

"Aha," he said as if a light bulb had gone off in head, "that's different; this must have been a private church. That was common during that time period for the very wealthy. How long will you be staying in Soccoro?"

"We're here only a few days," Danny replied. He told us to wait a few minutes as he disappeared into an office. Mr. Serrano photocopied a street map which had three red circles. He put the map on a table and said, "I know of three very old abandoned churches around out town. As you can see on this map two of these structures are several miles north of the town and the other one is here," as he pointed to a location on the eastern edge of town. "Try these places and maybe it's the church you're looking for but in the meantime, I will conduct a search through our archives which could take a bit of time."

"Wow that's awesome that you're willing to take the time to do this research for us, we'd like to pay you for your time."

He quickly replied, "No, no, it would be my pleasure to assist you and see if your information is correct. Where are you staying?"

"Duerma Bien Hotel," Danny replied.

"As soon as I finish my query I will leave a message for you at the hotel, is that OK?" We thanked him for his generous assistance and headed back to our truck.

We decided to try and find as many of the abandoned churches as possible. We resolved to drive to the eastern side of the town and then try for the others later, daylight permitting. The drive took just under two hours. The area was nothing more than open lands littered with junk yards interspersed with trailer homes. After slowly cruising the area, we found the dirt road as the map indicated. We proceeded reluctantly on the gravel path and within thirty minutes, there it was, a long forgotten hull of a church which nature and gravity had taken its toll on. The windows were shattered, doors hanging on the few threads of their hinges with trusses that could no longer support a roof. There was no indication that this was part of a massive estate but we got out of the truck and inspected the building. We found nothing to indicate the name of the church. We walked around to look for a massive tree and came up with diddly-squat! "This ain't it, let's hit the road," Danny said.

"Agreed, let's blow out of here."

The other churches on the map were both north of Soccoro. Danny had the driving duties today. I swear, during our northward push I almost told him to just keep on driving until we crossed the border back to the U.S. but like always, that mechanism inside of me kicks in and won't let me quit once I start something.

The map provided by Mr. Serrano was precise so we were certain we could find the other two abandoned churches. A few hours later we arrived at the northern part of Soccoro which was probably a town unto itself. The church was easy to spot sitting decrepit on the side of a major road. "No way, this church wasn't part of a wealthy estate. Another thing, dusk is just around the corner, why don't we regroup at the hotel," Danny suggested.

"10-4 partner, let's roll out of here," I said dejectedly!

We drove back to the center of town to get our bearings then back to the hotel and it was almost nightfall. That's the thing about this kind of work, when you're looking for treasure, hours of the hunt slip away by what seems like seconds. Then comes the down time where waiting for the next day in great anticipation, time moves so very slowly in what feels like an eternity.

Once back at the hotel we checked our rooms to make sure nothing had been stolen and retreated to the dining room. There we ordered steaks from Carmelita and had another outstanding dinner while planning our strategy for the next day. I hated to go back to my depressing room, my only solace was being able to exchange emails with Jean.

Day 2

Sure enough the next morning arrived and our plan was to continue searching for the last church listed on our map.

Northward we went and after several hours we found ourselves off roading again, inhaling choking dust, eventually finding the last abandoned church. The structure did not reveal anything indicating it was once a church! 'Bubkis' once again, nothing but shanty houses with tin roofs, dust and chocking polluted air. "Let's go back to the city center and get one of those giant tortas sandwiches, "Danny proposed!

"Yeah why not, nothing to see here."

We arrived in the town square and unlike American cities, we just parked our truck any damn place we wanted. Certainly no traffic enforcement in this place. We entered the little sidewalk restaurant, sat down and ordered our tortas and fries. The waitress brought our coffee and while waiting for our sandwiches we finally realized that our gringo appearance made us targets of a barrage of curious and hostile stares. "Town folks don't seem too happy to see a couple of tourista gringos," I said in a hushed voice.

"Agreed," Danny answered. We ate our gigantic chicken tortas and fries, paid the bill and beat feet out of there. As we walked toward our truck we noticed two men in their 30's leaning against a wall both just milling around suspiciously. One of them moved toward us and called out, "Jou Americans?"

I replied, "Yes, you speak English?"

"Si, of course, I speak very gude English, you want a little marijuana, hash?"

Danny stepped in and replied, "No we're . ." The man abruptly interrupted Danny,

"OK, OK, I can get cocaine, is that good for you? I'll include good woman, how you say, eh, a package deal?"

"I was getting tired of the fool but I tried one last time to get information from him since at least he spoke English, "Listen amigo, we don't want any of that shit. We are looking for the Iglesia de los Santos, do you know the location?"

He got an angry look on his face and retorted, "you buy our stuff then we take you to church." We weren't getting anywhere with these dudes so we walked away, at which point the man ran to Danny and grabbed his left arm. "Gringo you buy our stuff now, or we will impose a tax on youse for walking in our territory."

Out of reflex, Danny spun around and struck the man to the side of the head with his bear sized paw. The Mexican crumpled to the ground like a sack of flower.

His partner, who had simultaneously attempted to lunge at Danny, got a swift front kick from me to his stomach and I was able to easily pin him to the ground with my knee.

Danny rolled his assailant on his stomach and meticulously patted him down, "Sal, this guy's clean," he yelled out.

I did a cursory pat down on my guy and I yelled back at Danny, "no weapons here either!" I looked at the would be drug dealer who was stunned and informed, "you should be careful who you mess with, you're liable to get hurt, comprende?" The Mexican nodded, not offering any resistance. "Now go help your partner, I think he needs to go to the hospital."

Without saying anything else he got off the ground and walked over to his partner who was groggy from the palm strike. "Danny, let's make a bee line for the truck."

"OK, let's rock out of here!"

We double timed it back to our truck, periodically looking back making the sure the two bandits were not following us. As soon as we drove off, Danny turned toward me and lamented, "Man, I thought we agreed there'd be no drama on this trip?"

"I thought so too partner."

Danny looking straight ahead asked, "Hey, have you seen any type of police presence or patrol car anywhere?"

I thought about it for a few seconds and replied, "Now that you mention it, I haven't seen any police presence since we got to Soccoro."

"This place is definitely bad news partner," Danny mumbled. It was clear that the absence of any legal controlling authority in this town had given free rein to the cartels and their local feeder gangs.

It was now 5 PM, while driving back to the hotel, I was getting concerned and agitated that it was already day two and time was slipping away from us. Another fruitless day with absolutely nothing to show for our efforts except a run in with local drug dealers which is what we wanted to avoid at all costs.

Once we got to the hotel we checked to make sure our rooms had not been burglarized so we paid off the security guard and retreated back into our rooms. That evening while burning the midnight oil and perusing the state and city maps, I heard banging on the wall that I shared with Danny's room. The noise was Danny yelling up a storm, knocking roaches off the wall with his shoe. The mental picture in my head just made bust out laughing. I went back to working on tomorrow's strategy which made me oblivious to the roaches crawling all over my walls! Oh well, sometimes it pays to turn a blind eye on a bad situation!

Day 3

We had our breakfast very early and travelled to a town west of Soccoro with the strange name of Muelas de los Toros, or the molar teeth of bulls, which had in its town's center a 19th century church. Although this town was not mentioned in the Doc Benitez story, we decided to travel to the church and possibly pick up some relevant leads.

We drove westward for about four hours and arrived at the Capilla de la Virgen [*Chapel of the Virgin*]. The church had a parking lot surround by a five foot tall rock wall to which Danny remarked, "Man, this looks like a fort with a church in the middle!"

"Strange indeed, let's go in and see what we see!"

As we entered the church we were immediately greeted by a man who must have sized us up as gringos because he greeted us with, "Buenos dias, Señores, I am the rector of this church."

Me and Danny replied in unison, "Buenos dias."

"Welcome to our humble church gentlemen, how can I assist you?"

"I responded, "Sir, we are searching for the Hidalgo hacienda in Soccoro which had on the property a church named la Iglesia de los Santos, have you ever heard of this place?"

The Rector looked pensive for a few seconds and replied, "Well this region had several very large Haciendas in the 1800's and early 1900's but all of them were erased from the history books after the Mexican revolution. Over the years I've heard stories of several rich landowners who had large cattle farms in the Soccoro region but where exactly, I cannot say."

Struck out again so we thanked the Rector and began walking out with him in escort. While we walked he inquired as to why we were searching for such an obscure location. I quickly changed the subject and conveyed our delight and being able to visit his church, a true masterpiece of architectural design. The Rector seemed pleased that I appreciated the beauty of his church but as he fumbled with his rosary he got a concerned look on his face and implored us in a lowered tone, "Please listen to me, you look like decent men, take care of your business quickly, this region belongs to Cicatriz and his gang."

"Cicatriz, who's that," asked Danny?

The Rector shook his head in disbelief at our ignorance. "That man is a ruthless killer who has his own private army and runs the drug trade and human smuggling in this region. The police don't patrol in this town anymore." Me and Danny shot wary glances at each other, exactly what we had observed in the past two days.

The rector continued, "The military are the only ones with the firepower to prevent the gangs from taking over everything. Leave this place as soon as possible. I don't want the same things to happen to you as to the other strangers that have visited and vanished never to be seen again! No one is safe here!"

I replied, "Thank you sir, we will take your advice."

"Que dios los acompañe!" [May God keep you] were the last words uttered by the Rector. With that ominous warning, we exited the church and began walking to our truck.

We were about ten feet from our vehicle when the tranquility of the church grounds exploded with loud pops of gunfire as a suburban SUV crashed into the church parking lot entrance which was the only way out. Six men armed with AK-47's bailed out of the truck, took cover behind their vehicle firing furiously at military trucks that were attempting to close in on them.

Once the Mexican soldiers dismounted we saw several of them spin wildly then go down as they were hit with a fusillade of bullets. After a few minutes the soldiers got their stuff together and established their shooting positions then poured it on with their old G-3 rifles. Their automatic gunfire intensified, blowing out the windshield and front end of the cartel's crashed SUV. The cartel members continued retreating while the Mexican soldiers continued advancing causing the gang members to panic and begin moving backwards toward our pickup truck.

From our position we could see the church doors but making a run for it would expose us to gunfire. "What do you think," Danny asked breathing hard like he had just run 10 miles?

"We need to get away from the truck now, before those assholes peel away and use our truck for cover. Can you make it over the wall," I asked?

Danny roared, "Hell yes, let's go!" We sprinted about fifty yards to the back side of the parking lot and jumped over the five foot wall like we were young rookie cops again and to the other side. We duck walked in a crouch around the wall perimeter to avoid the gunfire but as soon as we turned the corner wham! We ran smack into a Mexican military foot patrol who immediately gun faced us with their rusted out G3 rifles.

With their comrades involved in an ongoing gunbattle, these soldiers were worked up and ready to shoot anyone who looked suspicious so when they yelled, "¡Alto! ¡ manos arriba no te muevas!" We didn't need a Spanish dictionary to know that it meant stop, put your, hands up, and don't move. We knew the routine, so before they even finished barking out their commands we threw our hands up, palms facing outward.

After complying with their orders, I responded in the calmest voice I could muster," ¡No dispares, somos americanos!" [*Don't shoot we're Americans*]. The soldiers got caught off-guard by my Spanglish but then shoved us against the wall, kicked our legs apart so we went with the program and assumed a felony pat down position.

Danny turned his head slightly toward me and dripping with sarcasm growled, "Good damn grief, you promised no drama . ." The soldiers immediately poked us with their rifles and muttered something which we assumed meant, shut up.

We were searched while in the pat down position and the soldiers finding no weapons or drugs seemed surprised. Although they looked in our wallets they put them back into our pockets saying nothing to us. In the meantime one of the soldiers keyed up his two way radio, "Comandante, ven pronto, tenemos dos Americanos detenidos." [*Commander, come quick we have two Americans detained*!]. The back and forth skirmish between the gang and soldiers had now fallen silent which most likely implied that the six cartel members were either dead, wounded and or captured.

We remained in the felony pat down position for about fifteen minutes until a Humvee with red lights and siren arrived noisily to a halt. A dark skinned officer jumped out triggering all the Mexican soldiers to stiffen and salute him. The officer approached the sergeant in charge and asked, "Estos son los dos Americanos?" [*These are the two Americans?*].

"Si capitan."

"¿Registraron dentro de su camioneta?" [*Did you search their truck?*].

"Si, pero no había armas ni drogas, el camión estaba limpio." [*Yes, we searched but we didn't find weapons nor drugs, the truck was clean*].

The officer ordered us in perfect English, "You two, turn around!" We slowly came off the wall and faced the officer. "You are Americans?"

We answered in unison "yes sir."

"I am Capitan Fernandez, I am the military commander for this sector. So what is it you're doing in our lovely town, buying or selling?"

"Buying or selling what," Danny replied with a look of bewilderment?

"I warn you two gringos, things are going to get very rough, very quickly, if you don't answer me with the truth.

Are you buying drugs or selling guns, it's one or the other?"

I replied, "Commander, no disrespect to you and your men but we are not criminals!"

"OK, Americano you two are not here on vacation, so what is it?"

My scheming coconut when into overdrive trying to think of something to get us out of this mess. Then like a bolt of lightning, I thought about what the church rector told me about the cartel leader in this region. "Sir, we're searching for a dangerous criminal wanted in America."

"And who is that?"

"We came to Soccoro to find cartel leader Cicatriz. We plan to arrest him and take back to America. Isn't that right Danny?"

With a concerned look on his face, Danny confirmed my tall tale, "That's right, we are here to take Cicatriz back to America."

"Are you DEA, FBI who?"

"Can we take our police badges from our pockets?" He nodded yes so we pulled our retired police badge and identification card and displayed them to the commander, hoping he wouldn't notice the word 'retired' on our badge.

"As you can see capitan, we're police officers!"

"OK, great Mr. policemen, where's the rest of your team?"

"There's no team just the two of us," I responded.

With an incredulous tone in his voice the commander thundered, "Just you two, here alone, without weapons, going to arrest Cicatriz?" With his hands on hips he threw back his head and let out a full throated laugh. The commander turned around and addressed the soldiers on the sidewalk and ones in the trucks with 50 caliber mounted machine guns.

"¡Soldados, estos dos Americanos, solos en nuestra ciudad y sin armas y sin asistencia, planean capturar el Jefe del Cartel de Juárez, El único "Cicatriz!" y devolverlo a América! Que cojones!, no?"

[*Soldiers, these two Americans, alone in our city and without weapons or assistance, plan to capture the head of the Juarez cartel, the one and only "Cicatriz" and then march him across the border to America! What balls?]*

The commander's speech resulted in huge laughter and guffaws from the soldiers in the streets and in the gun trucks.

"You two crazy Americans, listen to me, you have not broken any laws, YET! Do yourselves a favor, go home, enjoy yourselves in the land of plenty or just go to Disneyland. You won't find Cicatriz, he will find you and if he does, he and his men will cut you into hundreds of pieces and feed them to his prized pigs! We have enough problems in this town without having to worry about two American policemen. Remember I warned you!"

Turning to his soldiers he loudly commanded the military patrol "Vamanos!" [*Lets go*]. The military vehicles sped off while the foot patrol marched away frequently looking at back at us with a 'you guys are dead meat' look.

We hoofed it out of there and into the church parking lot and were very surprised to find it our truck intact with not one single bullet hole. The same couldn't be said for the cartel's SUV which had been cut to pieces by the soldier's fire. A flatbed truck was in the process of removing the SUV. We approached the scene then backed off as we saw the gory, blood splattered evidence of the carnage that just occurred.

"Man, I hope that bullshit you told the military commander about searching for that dude Cicatriz doesn't come back to bite us in the ass," Danny opined.

"Shit, it's the only thing I could think of to throw them off the scent of the real reason we're here." With that we shrugged our shoulders and headed back to our hotel in a gloomy mood as our hopes of a quick find was getting less and less likely.

On the way back to the hotel we did some serious soul searching whether or not to call it a loss and return home. That evening during dinner not much was said between us as we contemplated today's near lethal encounter. After three full days we had come up with absolutely nothing but trouble and dropping dollars and pesos. The really big setback was that our run-ins with drug dealers and the military obliterated our strategy of maintaining a low profile, our anonymity had been blown away. So it was no surprise that before we retreated to our room we both agreed that if we came up dry tomorrow we'd cut our plans short by one day, pull up stakes and exfiltrate our assess back across the border.

Day 4

The morning was filled with tense trepidation. We'd search here, there and everywhere and with thought in mind that this day would be our last shot before calling it quits, was too painful to even contemplate. Although returning home with empty pockets was a bummer, I knew I still had one other treasure hunt up my sleeve that could turn out to be the one huge payday.

We headed to the dining area for what was probably our last breakfast at the Duerma Bien Motel. While waiting for our food, the hotel manager Carlos walked up to us with a purpose, he excitedly informed us that a Señor Serrano called and left a message for us to please come to the library for very important information. We looked at each other and celebrated the news with a high-five, maybe, just maybe, our luck was changing! We thanked Carlos and slipped him a fiver.

We slammed down our breakfast and informed Carlos to hold our rooms for an open ended period and he responded with a big grin and a si Señores affirmation.

We peeled out of the parking lot with our truck tires squealing as we headed for the library. On the way there it became very clear, no matter if we drove straight, turned left or right, sped up or slowed down, there was always an SUV or pickup with tinted windows, keeping a respectful distance but certainly tailing our ass. At this point we didn't mind too much being tailed as we hoped it was the military or the police and not the bad guys. However, somewhere down the line we'd have to lose them if we ever hoped to locate the Hacienda and maybe even find where the crates were buried.

Upon our arrival at the library, Mr. Serrano greeted us with a big smile. "Gentlemen, I believe I found the location you are looking for."

"Great, let's see what you found," I replied.

"Yes, follow me." We followed Mr. Serrano to a back office where a map was spread out over a long rectangular table. "After much research I found the Hidalgo family in our archives. A very wealthy family that seemed to have vanished sometime in the early 1900's," he paused for a second then continued, "Eh, this was not unusual as there were radical land reform changes during that time due to the revolution."

Danny replied, "So you have an idea where the property is located?"

"Yes, come here and take a look at this map." Me and Danny gave each other power fists in the air, finally confirming these two dudes really existed! Mr. Serrano showed us on the map all the places that we had searched and how we had missed the former Hidalgo property. We thanked Mr. Serrano effusively and offered again to pay him for his assistance which he politely but firmly rejected.

With our new map in hand we quickly departed the city center and began the journey through the narrow, winding roads out of the city. Soon enough we were surrounded by desolate desert scrubland and areas that once upon a time were fields of grazing cattle and sheep. The good part of this desolation was that our surveillance vehicles were nowhere to be seen!

We followed the map for approximately three hours moving southwest of Soccoro where our progress slowed down as the roads became less civilized.

It turned out to be a smart play renting a four wheel drive truck as we pushed deeper into the nearly impassable path where the sky was periodically replaced by a canopy that darkened the way forward.

With no guarantees that continuing on would lead us to the fabled Hidalgo hacienda, occasionally we'd shoot glances of doubt at each other, like what the hell are we doing here.

After a seemingly endless amount of time getting slammed back and forth on the rocky trail of sharp rocks, abruptly the thick canopy began to lessen and more of the sun's rays began peeking through. Soon enough, full daylight and in front of our windshield, a rotting, wooden ranch archway entrance with a faded double H metal sign hanging on the wood post. "Holy shit, double H, the Hidalgo Bros," I yelled out!

"Whoa, these dudes really existed," Danny muttered as he stared in disbelief at the archway.

"Brother, let's find the church and the tree," I said with renewed confidence.

Under the rickety wooden archway was a dual iron gate which was probably a formidable barrier several hundred years ago but now it was nothing more than a rusty, tetanus infested chunk of iron. We got out of the truck and pushed the gates open as they eerily screeched in disapproval!

We pushed through the gates that offered no further resistance and slowly drove along a winding driveway that at one time was a majestic corridor but now nothing more than a scarred cobblestone path with grass and weeds growing between the stones.

Within fifteen minutes, more confirmation of the story as we came upon the remains of a staggering Hacienda mansion. We slung our backpacks that contained our folding shovels and assorted supplies, as well as our lone metal detector and began walking. The long forgotten masonry corpse that was left to die alone, with no one to care for it came into view more clearly. The once milky white walls were now a brownish-black ugliness as the wind whistled through the broken windows and up through the collapsed roof. The good news about the hacienda was its location, far from civilization and prying eyes, or so we imagined!

As we circled to the rear, about two-hundred yards away were the remains of another building we hoped was the fabled Hidalgo private church. The structure was barely visible as it was encased by dense growth of scrub brush and prickly trees.

"Let's hope that's the church," I said as we both began fast walking toward the structure. As we neared the structure we removed our machetes from our backpacks and began hacking our way to the walls. We peeked inside through the window opening that had long ago shed its majestic stained glass. We observed a few remnants of the roof which had totally collapsed into the floor. As we moved around to the front of the church, barely hanging on by its hinges were two heavy wooden doors. Over the doorway we observed a much rusted ornamental metallic plate. Clearly visible was the engravings of,' IGLES' something, something, followed by SANTOS, no doubt about it, even though several letters were missing this clearly was the Iglesia de los Santos! "Damn," I yelled out! "This is it, everything in the story is here in front of us," I exclaimed!

"Damn, this is looking good Sal," Danny said amazed.

All was looking good, we'd checked off several boxes in confirmation of the Doc Benitez story but the elation was short lived. as we felt a familiar shooting range crunch of brass shell casings under our feet.

We were so focused on looking around for landmarks that we'd gotten a bad case of tunnel vision. We neglected to notice the ground beneath our feet was littered with empty shell casings, some tarnished but many others still glittering like gold, just not the gold we wanted to find! We picked up several shells and to our alarm, "7.62 x 39, how about you," I whispered with a sinking feeling of lurking danger.

Danny replied, "Same here but also some 5.56, hell Sal, I think these people were hunting big game, the two legged type for sure."

Me and Danny were thinking the same thing, if the folks who had been doing the shooting at this location decided show up, we'd be extremely vulnerable without weapons. So, in the blink of an eye our mood changed from excitement to apprehension, oh well, we're this close, onwards, I thought to myself.

As we walked to the other side of the church we got another surprise, submerged in the grass and weeds was a graveyard but no giant tree visible anywhere. Danny immediately pointed out the obvious, "Hey, if this is the church in the story, shouldn't we have seen by now a giant tree that was the size of a building?"

"Damn, no tree," as my voice trailed off in disbelief. While still looking around dumbfounded, I exclaimed to no one in particular, "Doc Benitez never said anything about a cemetery near the church!"

Hell, maybe after one-hundred years of retelling the story the actual location of the crates was wildly inaccurate. That annoying little voice kept tugging at me that we might have to return home empty handed. So the only response I had for Danny was, "I'm sure we're at the right place!"

Our three goals for this trip was at a minimum, confirm the existence of the Hacienda, find the church and the tree then return at a later date to recover the horde. So with no giant tree in sight two out of three was still not good enough to confirm Doc Benitez's story.

As we surveyed the dreary abandoned landscape, I called out, "alright, we've got our job cut out for us, let's start walking a grid pattern and see what's what?"

"Copy, let's get to it," Danny said with a sigh signaling his pessimism that we were close to finding a shitload of gold.

After about one hour of looking around the first section of the cemetery, which was mostly clear of brush, we encountered headstones that had been ravaged by the wind and rain and in many cases the names, dates and remembrances had been erased as if that person never existed. From the headstones that were readable we concluded the dead were interned sometime between the 1920's to the 1950s, well after the Hidalgo brothers had abandoned the property in 1914.

Danny being a smart ass chimed in, "Hey, with these folks being buried all over the place maybe some undertakers hit the jackpot when they were burying Pepe."

"Sure hope not," I quipped with the sick realization that it was plausible.

We trudged up and down, through dense brush with roots, thorns and thickets tearing and tugging at us obstructing our every step as if the graveyard was telling us to go away. With no sign of the giant tree or where it may have stood, we sat down on an old, rickety wooden bench on the edge of the cemetery. We plucked thorns and brushed crap off our clothes while we pondered our options as visions of glittering gold were disappearing by the second. "Everything has checked out, the Hidalgo Hacienda, the church, so where the hell is that tree," I muttered?

Danny rubbing his chin responded, "Hey, let's get on with this and finish checking that last quadrant of the cemetery. If we find nothing we'll beat feet back to the hotel, get our shit and go home, what do you think?"

"Yeah, it sucks that we've come this far and may have to leave empty handed but it makes sense brother" I replied with sagging shoulders and disappointment etched on my face.

We leapt up of the bench and I slapped Danny on the back," C'mon man, you take the west side and I'll take the east and we'll meet in the middle. Let's find this shit, ay!" With that said and a bit of a bounce in our step we began the end of our search.

We separated to opposite ends of the graveyard and began a meticulous search. We trekked through the dense scrub brush and weeds looking for any terrain markers, any sign that said, here stood a giant behemoth I mused to myself in quiet despair!

We were separated by about fifty yards of the rectangular patch of land yet to be searched. We always kept an eye on each other, a tactic acquired from many years of undercover police assignments. So, when I glanced sideways and didn't see the big Irishman, I called out, " Danny, you alright?" I could hear Danny cussing up a storm but I couldn't determine his location. I rushed to where I saw him last and I heard Danny's tone change from pissed off to excited, "Hey, get your ass over here," Danny yelled out.

"Coming," I screamed out as I moved as fast as possible considering the thorns and twigs tearing into my clothes which was hampering my movement. At first I assumed Danny had done a face plant into a grave and might be hurt but once I reached him I realized what the excitement was all about as I stared wide eyed at the gargantuan tree stump and roots. "This gotta be the tree Doc Benitez told you about," Danny blurted out.

Breathing hard from my struggle against the unruly scrub brush, I said in a gasping voice, "shit, shit, you're right, this gotta be the tree, it just has to be."

"What are we waiting for," Danny asserted with uncharacteristic enthusiasm.

12

MILLION DOLLAR MOMENT

Be patient Buried Treasure, wait a little longer while I search for you, I will find you and let you out to see the light of day once again. - Unknown

It was now 5:30 PM, the sky in the horizon was a shade of pinkish orange so we figured we had less than one hour before the deadline of daylight gave way to darkness on this partly cloudy March day.

The benchmarks of locating the three landmarks had now been accomplished so this trip's goals had been met but it was only fair to let Danny decide whether we should take off and come back another time. "Danny, want to leave now and come back at another time or do you want to do a little metal detecting?"

I guess that unstoppable force of nature when it comes to treasure hunting had definitely infected Danny because he surprisingly responded, "Hell Sal, we're come this far, I think we're safe for now, let's see if we can find the crates!"

"Oorah, let's get it done," I yelled.

According to the account by Doc Benitez, the crates were buried ten paces from the giant tree but in what direction was unknown. Resolute and determined, we strategized to conduct a slow, outward spiral search with our metal detector in opposite directions from the base of the skeletal remnants of what had once been a majestic giant tree. Within no time flat, a blanket of inky blackness smothered the graveyard which felt menacingly primal. We decided that Danny would continue sweeping the ground with his detector while I followed him with a flashlight.

We pushed on as eerie shadows danced around the tombstones from the clouds moving across the moon. I guess we'd watched too many horror movies because at times it felt like a bony skeletal arm would emerge from the soil and grab our legs which rattled even us two veteran street cops.

The heavy brush continuously tangled around the coil of Danny's detector, impeding his sweeping motion, slowing our search to a crawl. The advantage we had was that our detector had a large coil that was set on a discrimination mode for deeper objects saving us huge amounts of time and frustration digging up useless shallow targets that were likely nails, cans and other metallic trash.

After several hours of back breaking nothingness with the detector, Danny's Irish luck materialized just like a leprechaun and his pot-O-gold at the end of the rainbow. In a hushed tone Danny called out, "Whoa! got a really strong signal here!" I shined the light at the exact location of the hit then Danny put the detector on the ground, we removed the machetes from our backpacks and began hacking away the brush before we got to digging.

Once we identified the correct area we got to digging right away. After digging out a three foot section which was about one foot deep we swept the detector coil over the section. There was no doubt about it, the target was under our feet!

We continued digging feverishly but at the two foot depth, still nothing. We took turns widening our search circumference and it was the same old treasure hunting story, perhaps it's here, perhaps it's there, perhaps a few feet deeper! Exasperated I called out, "Danny, are we getting a ghost signal or what?"

"Hold on let me pass the coil over the hole again." Danny picked up the detector and swept the coil several times over the gaping hole, "Whatever the hell it is, it's still below our feet, the sound is solid and even stronger now" Danny said authoritatively.

With those words ringing in my ear I told Danny to step out of the hole to give me more room and began attacking the ground with new fervor. Every muscle in my body knotted up at the realization that if our target turned out to be a buried 57 Chevy engine, we'd be on the road home with empty pockets and a sore muscles!

But before too long at about the three foot deep level my shovel struck a solid object with a thud. I thrust my shovel in several different locations trying to figure out the shape of the object, it definitely had symmetry to it, a crate I screamed in my head!

Danny couldn't wait any longer and yelled out in a whisper, "I heard that, let me get some more light in there."

Suddenly it dawned on me and I muttered, "Damn, I hope it's not a casket!"

Danny's respond was quick, "No way man, we're only about three feet down."

Although exhausted and drenched in sweat I went after the hole like a New York City grave digger!

About half an hour later Danny demanded, "c'mon now, it's big enough in there for you to crawl around and figure out what we have."

As I widened the area I could finally see the outline of a box like object. With my heart pounding, I began scooping and scraping the dirt away from the top of the object with my hands. I got a disgusting feeling when I felt a metal curvature, "Oh shit, I think it's a coffin or some type of ossuary box for the bones."

"Can you open it?" Danny urged impatiently.

"Hit me with more light!" I replied.

Danny pulled out the long strip lighting from his backpack and lit up the hole which clearly showed the box was metallic and not wood.

"Shit I think I've seen this kind of box in antiques stores, it's an iron armada type chest," I reported to Danny.

"Is that good?"

"Hell yes it's good!"

If this wasn't a burial ossuary then this crate or chest was in remarkable condition with metal handles on each side that appeared to be intact. The box had two separate hasps for padlocks but no locks. I furiously wiped away dirt and debris with my hands until the separation between the crate and the lid was exposed. I yanked and pulled to no avail. I banged the chest with my shovel then stuck the shovel blade between the lid and the crate to pry the lid open which did so with a hideous creaking sound as the lid surrendered its hold on the secrets that lay inside. I wiped off a coating of dust and debris inside the crate and called out to Danny, "point your light more to my left!"

Then, total sensory overload as the waning power of Danny's lightstrip cast a cloudy beam on the opened crate which released a yellow glow within the excavated hole. For what seemed like an eternity I was frozen with my mouth open. I now knew how British archaeologist Howard Carter felt when he peeked into the burial chamber of Tutankhamun and responded to the inquiring throng behind him asking what he saw, '*wonderful things.*'

This metal crate which hadn't seen the light of day in nearly one hundred years, lay undisturbed in silence waiting for me and Danny's arrival. As I scooped my hand inside the crate, indeed there were wonderful things! I took a deep breath to gather myself and finally found my voice, "Holy shit, oh my God, pay dirt Danny, it's here, it's all here," I yelled out!

"Get out of the way, let me get in there." Danny gave me a hand up and pulled me out of the hole then he jumped in. He screamed and whooped like a crazy person as he hysterically scooped up handfuls of coins and put some in his pockets. I couldn't help laughing out loud at the sight of my partner trying to fill his pockets with the coins but I brought him back to reality.

"Forget taking samples just keep digging out that hole so we can remove one or two of the crates tonight if possible!"

We worked hurriedly to widen the hole so that we both could fit into the ditch. We cleared out about one foot to the left of the chest which quickly unearthed a second crate. "Man oh man it's all here, the story was real all along," I screamed out with a bit of disbelief!

Danny picked up on that immediately, "Why, you had doubts that this was nothing more than a fairy tale? Yet you dragged me to this shit hole of a town?"

I laughed it off and replied, "I knew the treasure was real," as I rolled my eyes internally!

For the next couple of hours we widened the ditch and exposed the top two crates. We surmised that all the crates were piled in rows of four crates stacked on top of each other in a near perfect trench line. Damn, those Franciscan monks were efficient excavators I kept thinking to myself. We hoisted the top crate out of the hole and examined the contents more closely. "Danny, I think there's a lot more than five hundred coins in these chests and look, they're mostly gold!"

Danny excitedly implored, "Outstanding, let's dig out the second one before daybreak.

"Let's do it. We'll get the two crates into the truck, cover the hole with dirt and scrub brush then we'll come back tomorrow night and recover a few more."

"You know Sal, maybe we shouldn't wait to get all the crates out. Why don't we extend our stay in Soccoro, get all the crates out and secure them in that self-storage facility in Hermosillo?"

"Hey man you're right, why wait and have someone stumble on to our gold, lets stay in Soccoro as long as necessary till we get them all out and safely stored!"

With that new plan in place, we busily began digging out the second crate and examining the outlines of the other crates still ensconced in the dirt. We were so damned focused and engrossed trying to calculate the millions of dollars underneath us that we altogether lost all situational awareness and let our guard down. On account of, out of nowhere, came a murmur of voices just out of our line of sight. Then we heard an ominous voice say, "Hola Americanos, what jou looking for?" as we heard laughter from other men. We looked up from our ditch and saw the dim figures of four men armed with AK47's, which caused my oh-shit gauge to swerve into the red zone. For a few breathless moments we stood dazzled on the threshold of a fortune and now that strangely familiar feeling of trouble and riches slipping through our fingers!

"What now?" Danny said in a hushed voice.

"Play it cool, let's try and take em when we get out of the ditch."

In a hushed scream Danny said, "You crazy, they'll cut us to pieces with their automatic weapons, let's wait and see when we have a better chance to escape."

"Jou looking for Cicatriz in deer?" as the laughter continued from the other men. "Don't worry, we take you to him. Now come out of hole with jour hands up, Jou two have an appointment with the big boss!" I was all out frantic trying to figure a way out of this tight spot but knew that one wrong move would be instant death for the two of us.

As soon as we got out of the ditch two of the bandits slithered around to our rear and slapped the side of our heads with the flat side of their

AK-47 wood stocks. We fell to the ground facedown and although not badly injured, I whispered to Danny, "Just stay down like we're stunned." Our wrists were quickly and forcefully tied behind our backs with plastic zip ties, so it was clear these dudes had done this many times before. Inexplicably, out of the blue, six other gang members arrived and a furious back and forth argument ensued, most likely about the gold that was no longer in our possession. Danny leaned over to me and said in muted voice, "What d'ya think, they gonna kill us?"

"Probably!"

"Damn, I shouldn't have asked!"

The arguing between the two groups escalated to a pushing, shoving match and occasionally pointing their weapons at each other. But as suddenly as it began, the cartel brainstorming session abruptly ended, I guess they came to some type of agreement. Four of the six men from the second group picked us up and threw us into the rear of the pickup truck while the two others stayed with the original four men.

The truck sped off, and within a minute or two we heard automatic weapons fire emanating from the direction of the graveyard. The two men guarding us talked excitedly in Spanish and shook hands as if something great had occurred. We were laying on the floor of the truck with our hands tied behind our backs and a AK-47 sized headache. I took the opportunity to check on Danny while the guards bantered back and forth,

"You OK?"

Breathing heavily and unevenly, "I've been better Sal. You know what gnaws at me?" taking in some deep breaths, "we were home!" pausing again Danny took an indrawn breath and continued, "We had our pensions, a decent chunk of change from Afghanistan! Dammit, I think our lucky streak has run out!"

The gang members realized we were communicating and one of them pulled Danny's head up by his hair and angrily threatened him, "Hey Cabrón [bastard] shut up or you'll get more Soccoro justice." Like Manna from heaven, Danny's Irish luck materialized once again. The guard did a double take when he saw Danny's face and he loudly remarked, "¡No mames!" [*Holy Shit*]. He stammered in disbelief, "Hey, you the cops that stopped me right? Back in America, right? Yeah, yeah, it was last Christmas, remember? Que locura!" [*What a crazy coincidence?*]. "yeah, you let me go after I put my very expensive Desert Eagle on the ground! You know, I really miss that gun!"

Not knowing if this was a good memory or if this dude was extra pissed that we confiscated his weapon, Danny carefully replied, "Good God, yeah, I remember. We helped you out big time that night. You're Manuel, El Caballo, right?"

"Si. Amigo it's me but you two are in deep shit."

With few precious seconds to figure a way to escape with our heads attached to our torsos, I jumped in. "Manuel can you help us out?"

Manuel paused and got the look of a man who had just got a brainstorm because to my utter shock he replied,

"Look, you two saved me that night so I owe you. You'll find out that Manuel always pays back his debts! So I got a plan in which you guys are going to help me again and then I will repay my debt by getting you both out of this mess." He grabbed his comrade on the shoulders and gave him a shake, "This is my cousin Jorge," who flashed a friendly smile all the while pointing his M4 at our heads. Manuel pointed at the two men in the driver's compartment and informed us they were also part of his posse. He went on to outline how things worked in the cartel. Manuel had his own gang that Cicatriz frequently used for critical operations in México and in the United States. He concluded by angrily complaining, "We're tired of Cicatriz's double dealing bullshit. We know he's going to keep all that gold for him and his family! We won't get one stinking coin, but we have other plans for that gold."

"OK great news for you Manuel but how are you going to get us out of here?" I countered with great urgency.

Danny, who was also frantic and wanting to get the zip ties cut off our wrists roared at Manuel, "C'mon man, cut us loose!"

Manuel and Jorge propped us up into a sitting position rather than lying on our sides like hogs going to the slaughter house. Manuel calmly replied, "Here's my problem, if I kill Cicatriz I'll have an army of Cicatriz's men seeking retribution, me and my family would never get to enjoy a minute of peace, so here's my offer. If we help you escape, are you willing to take that Cabrón across the border and turn him over to the DEA, FBI CIA, whoever, so that he'll never set foot in México again?"

I confidently assured him, "Mannie, you get us out of this mess, I'll carry the asshole across the border on my back! We'll make sure he never returns to México. Now c'mon, cut us loose!"

"No, not here, let's wait till we get to the farm house so we can get our hands on Cicatriz."

"You sure about this Mannie?" Danny asked.

"Hey, I'm risking everything! My life, my cousin's life and my entire posse's life! We want that piece of shit Cicatriz out of México. That bastard is bringing terrorists from other countries into México and helping them get across the border into America. He's making a ton of money but it's bringing a lot of heat on us from Mexican and American Federal police. Many of our members have been arrested and extradited to America because of that stupid greedy asshole!"

We agreed to remain with our hands bound behind our backs and cautiously go along with Manuel's plan, just no other options for us.

From what I could discern, we were being driven northward toward Magdalena, a mere speck on the map and last town before the U.S. border. Although we were in a shitload of trouble, the thought of being so close to the U.S. border somehow gave me a sense of comfort. I figured if we somehow escaped, the adrenaline rush would propel us like 'The Flash' at the speed of light to the border crossing.

The pickup truck pulled off the main road and we travelled for a couple of miles on a bumpy dirt road before arriving at the entrance of a farm that was guarded by two armed cartel members. Manuel and his posse greeted the men who waived us through. We ambled on the farm road and stopped in front of a small cement bock house with a front door and no windows.

As we were ushered into the structure, an immediate odor of rot hit us followed by an overwhelming feeling that this claustrophobic cinder block box held captive screams of pain and death. Me and Danny hesitated at the doorway but Manuel gave us a slight bump to get us in and said, "Don't worry we'll get you out of here alive!" What the hell could we do anyway, so we entered the room and observed a long dark wooden table with assorted bottles of tequila along with ropes, zip ties, knives and two chainsaws. I gotta admit, I've been scared many times in my life but I can't recall ever being more scared as my imagination went into overdrive thinking of the horrors that could befall us.

Manuel's men sat us in tall wooden chairs and proceeded to use the ropes on the table to lash us tight. I protested out loud, "Hey, what kind of bullshit is this?"

Danny also chimed in, "What the hell is going on Mannie?"

Manuel confidently assured us, "Listen to me, just keep cool, my plan will work, if not, we're all dead!" When Manuel first told us his plan I was apprehensive but now I was beyond alarmed. Our life was on the line on the word of a drug cartel member, if there ever was a time for prayer to the almighty, this was it!

Manuel ordered the two members of his crew to stand guard outside the building and to inform him when they saw Cicatriz approaching. Mannie and his cousin Jorge stayed inside with us all the while toting deadly high tech M4's with Aimpoint scopes and flashlight laser combo illumination. During the long drawn-out wait for Manuel's plan to unfold, me and Danny occasionally shot glances at each other as we looked on with great apprehension. Terrible thoughts entered my head as to what lay ahead for us. I kept running possible scenarios through my head. One thing I was sure of, Manny's plan had more holes in it than Swiss cheese but we were hopelessly trapped in someone else's plan so there was nothing I could do to change the dynamics of our shitty predicament.

Abruptly, Manuel's cell phone rang interrupting the deadly silence of the cement torture chamber. Manuel spoke briefly to what I assumed was a member of his gang because he ended his call with a Bueno! Perfecto! Then said to us, "Everything is working perfectly amigos, just hang in there till the bastard arrives. A ray of hope I thought! Suddenly one of the men outside the building opened the door, partially stuck his head into the room and with a look of terror on his face, blurted out, "Él Cabrón está aquí!" [The bastard is here]. He quickly closed the door and posted up outside the building.

A Ford Explorer SUV with blacked out tinted windows pulled up to the building and two bodyguards got out quickly. The driver ran to the door of the cement structure, exchanged a few words with Manuel's guards then motioned to the bodyguard in the SUV that it was clear. The bodyguard opened the door and Cicatriz exited the vehicle as if he was a head of state. Once out, Cicatriz strutted to the front door and asked the guards, "Los policías Americanos están adentro? [*The two Americans are inside*].

"Si Jefe!" [*Yes boss*] replied one of Manuel's guards with a hint of fear in his voice.

Cicatriz blurted out in an emotionless manner to no one in particular, "Es hora de cortar a los Americanos y alimentar mis puercos!" [*It's time to slice and dice the Americans and feed them to my pigs*]. Upon entering, Cicatriz ordered Manuel's men to remain outside.

Cicatriz entered the room with his two bodyguards and noticed us seated and lashed to the wooden chairs. He looked at Manuel and Jorge and told them to wait outside. Manuel and his cousin nodded and walked out of the room but gave us a look which I hoped was a hang in there look and not goodbye suckers look. Cicatriz was nothing of how I pictured the big boss to look like. It was obvious how he got the nickname Cicatriz as the long jagged, red scar that snaked down the left side of his face became visible. However, he was a short, squat, over weight, rotund man, wearing a soccer team jersey, blue jeans and cowboy boots, not quite the 'Mister Big' look.

"Hello gringos, a little birdie told me that two gringo policemen are searching for me in town and were going to arrest me, take me back to America, is that so?"

I quickly replied, that we were retired cops and that no, we didn't even know who he was when we came to Socorro in search for the crates of coins!

Cicatriz smiled and said, "Well you found the crates, congratulations and now the gold is mine. That was very Anglo of you!" which brought laughter from his bodyguards who up to that point stood around like wooden mannequins. "You pinche [*goddamned*] Americanos have Disneyland, social security and welfare but you come to our poor nation to steal our gold, that's greedy! Now tell me what agency you with, DEA? CIA?"

In a Hail Mary attempt, Danny responded, "You got bad information, we cane to Soccoro for the gold only, we have nothing to do with the U.S. Government."

Cicatriz went quiet and had a pensive expression as if he was actually thinking about letting us go but he then answered with, "Well, maybe yes, but the truth is you come to my home territory and make the soldiers and police cause more problems for me!"

Cicatriz walked up and slapped me on the side of the head and said, "Gringo, that was just an attention getter, you look like you need a shave!" Cicatriz walked away and headed to the table and before you can scream KNIFE, he grabbed the biggest, menacing cutting instrument on the table and once again advanced toward me for what appeared to be the kill. With a menacing grimace on his face he calmly said, "It's dinner time for my hungry puercos who like to eat American ears, si?" The bodyguards dutifully laughed out heartily.

I was frantic, as was Danny, where the hell was Manuel, so as Cicatriz approached me with knife in hand, me and Danny screamed out, "Caballo Now! Hurry! Now!" Cicatriz hesitated and froze as did his bodyguards for the split second needed for Manuel and Jorge to burst through the door. Both men entered with their M-4's in a modified high ready position and got on target in a zeptosecond firing only two precision shots at the bodyguards whose heads recoiled from the bullet's impact spraying blood everywhere. I know our lives were still in peril but the first thought that came to my mind was, damn, those two boys are great shooters!

Cicatriz was shocked at what just happened but with a surge of savage anger, he screamed, "Pendejos!" [*Bastards*] and ferociously charged past Jorge and towards Manuel with knife in hand. Jorge sidestepped the charging Cicatriz and butt stroked him the back of the head with his M4, sending him sprawling to the ground and stunned into silence. Manuel ordered Jorge to get the zip ties and strap that asshole's hands behind his back and to stuff a rag in his mouth.

Although Danny was fully aware that we were at the mercy of these two killers, he was still pissed that he was almost cut to pieces but still snapped at Manuel, "C'mon Manuel! Dammit, hurry up, untie us!"

Manuel ran to Danny and cut him loose then cut the ropes that were binding me to my chair.

"What the hell took you so long?" I asked with a half pissed, half relieved tone."

Manuel didn't answer me as he ran to the dead bodyguards. He rummaged through the dead man's pockets and retrieved the keys to Cicatriz's SUV. He promptly gave the keys to the two gang members who were now at the threshold of the opened door. Manuel ordered them to quickly get the SUV and stage it just outside the cement structure in order to facilitate a hasty exit from the farm.

As soon as the SUV was staged, Manuel, his cousin and the other two men picked up the dead bodyguards and quickly carried them outside and threw them on the floor board of the SUV then covered them with blanket all the while me and Danny kept an eye on Cicatriz. Manuel came back into the room and began wiping the bloody mess on the floor with rags, I turned toward Danny and whispered, "Maybe they like keeping the torture room clean!"

Unexpectedly and without provocation, Manuel and Jorge walked over to Cicatriz who was still groggy and each of them struck him with the butt of their rifle and chided him, "Buenas noches Cabrón!" It was clear that these men had a deep seated hatred for Cicatriz and definitely did not play around. They then wrapped Cicatriz in a blanket then hustled him outside and dumped him on top of the dead bodyguards.

Manuel instructed the two men to drive quickly out of the compound and not stop for anyone, which was customary for Cicatriz whenever he departed the farmhouse. He further instructed them to wait for us at a designated location near the border familiar to the gang. The two men promptly departed the farm in Cicatriz's SUV at a high rate of speed and none of the cartel members dared to stop or question them.

In the meantime Jorge brought the pickup truck that we were transported to the farm and parked it at the door step of the cement house. Manuel walked to us with the bloody rags and advised, "Sorry but I have to wipe this shit all over your heads."

"What the hell for?" I demanded to know.

"Just do as I say, lay on the floor and play dead, quickly, c'mon move fast before that asshole's men show up!"

With our lives still in mortal peril, we lay on the floor as instructed then Manuel proceeded to smear the warm, nasty bloody goo all over our head and face, enough to make us gag. They first carried me to the truck with ease but they really struggled to get the big Irishman into the truck. With both of us in the bed of the truck, Manuel firmly told us, "If you want to get out of this farm alive, play dead until we get out of the compound!"

We sped off making our way through the farm road but were stopped near the exit gates by a group of armed gang members. The leader of this group asked Manuel what was going on because they heard gunfire then saw Cicatriz leaving in a big hurry.

Manuel responded, "Si, matamos a los dos Americanos. Cicatriz nos ordenó abandonar los cuerpos sobre la frontera. Cicatriz fue a la ciudad con sus guardaespaldas. Van a secuestrar a los otros dos policias Americanos. Quiere que te reúnas con él en su hotel y lo ayudes a agarrar a los dos Americanos y llevarlos de vuelta a la granja!

[*We shot both Americans. Cicatriz ordered us to throw the bodies across the border. Cicatriz went to the city with his* bodyguards. They're going to abduct two other American policemen working with the two we have in the back. He wants your posse to meet him at his hotel and help snatch the two other American policemen then bring them back to the farm house].

The lead gang member walked around to the bed of the pickup and saw us lying in the back. He walked back to the driver's side and commented, "Que buenos, dos muertos Americanos." as he grinned. [Excellent! Two more dead Americans].

He then angrily said to Manuel, "¿Por qué carajo no nos dijiste eso antes, nos vamos ahora antes de que Cicatriz se enoje con nosotros!"

[Why the hell didn't you tell us this before? We're leaving now before Cicatriz gets pissed with us!]

The gang members all piled into a nearby SUV and sped off heading to the downtown Soccoro hotel owned by Cicatriz. Manuel gave Jorge a we just dodged a bullet look of relief and sped off for the border.

Once we were a few miles down the road, Manual stopped the pickup and came around to the bed of the truck. Apologetically he informed us that it was now clear to stop playing dead and move into the truck passenger compartment. As soon as we got in the truck, a huge blanket of relief swept over us. As we took off, me and

Danny grabbed Mannie and Jorge by the shoulders and thanked them. They gave us a thumbs-up as me and Danny celebrated with a double high-five.

As we continued northwest, Manuel received a call on his cell phone, "Bueno? Entonces tienes todos los cofres en nuestra ubicación, ¡Bien hecho! Mantente en contacto!" [*Hello, you've got all the crates at our location? Well done*!] "Regresaré a tu ubicación en breve." [*I'll get back to your location quick shit, stay in touch*!]

Turning to his cousin seated next to him. "Primo! ¡Lo tenemos! ¡Tenemos todos los cofres ¡Es la hora de comenzar una nueva vida, una vida tranquila!"

[*Cousin! We have it! We've got all the crates! it's time to start a new peaceful and tranquil life!*].

Jorge grabbed Manuel's shoulder and rejoiced, "Lo hicimos, podemos dejar este boyuyu, Dios está con nosotros! ¡Una nueva vida para mi esposa e niños!" [*We did it, God is with us! A new start for my wife and children away from all this chaos!*].

Eventually, we arrived in a really sketchy deserted area near the Mexican-U.S. border consisting of narrow foot paths pocked with scrub brush, cactus and trash strewn everywhere. Although we were still euphoric at escaping the cement house of death, it was clear that we were dealing with prolific killers and never let our guard down ever again. Even though we were acting like life-long friends with Manuel and Jorge, we'd have to be prepared to take them at the first hint that his plan was going off-course.

The SUV with Manuel's men, the two dead bodyguards and Cicatriz were already at the scene waiting. With great urgency Manuel ordered the men to get Cicatriz out of the SUV and throw him on the ground. The two men, with great disdain, dragged Cicatriz out of the truck and threw him to the ground like a fifty pound bag of rice.

With great precision, Manuel spit out his plan in rapid fire and ordered his men to bury the two bodyguards behind the scrub brush just off the goat trail. Manuel then announced, "Cicatriz's gang will assume that he and his bodyguards were arrested in Soccoro and taken to America by the other two policemen we invented," he said with a grin.

Wanting to show solidarity with Manuel, Danny chimed in, "Sounds like a helluva plan Manuel."

"Yep, and as soon as the two bodyguards are buried we'll set the SUV on fire leaving no trace of what happened here today!" Manuel asserted.

Now that we were relatively safe and in a holding pattern while the bodies were disposed I wanted to find out what the hell Manuel was doing on that cold Christmas night near the U.S. Capitol building. "Manuel, I just got to know! What the hell were you doing that night we stopped you in D.C.?" I asked.

"Yeah and why were you were carrying that damn cannon of a gun! What the hell was that all about?" Danny also inquired.

Manuel grinning slyly responded, "Well, I guess at this point it doesn't matter, with the gold we have stashed I won't be getting involved in that crazy shit ever again! Yeah, that night I was in D.C. at the designated location I always go to waiting for a staff member of a very powerful American politician. This staff member was delivering four American passports for some Middle Eastern dudes that were holed up in México. Like I told you before, Cicatriz is moving these Middle East guys into México, they get these legit American passports or green cards then cross into the U.S. with completely legit documents."

"What's the name of this politician?" Danny asked incredulously.

"No clue!" he answered.

"Are these folks wealthy and just want to live in America or is it something else?" I asked.

"Well, just from bits and pieces I've heard, these dudes are going across the border to create big trouble in your country. That man there," pointing to Cicatriz, "he knows how to buy services from politicians not only in México but also in your America."

"Damn! How many times have you done that?" I asked.

"That was my fourth trip so I estimate maybe twenty or so passports and maybe six green cards that I've picked up and transported back to Cicatriz in México."

"So, did you get to meet that staff member and make the delivery?" inquired Danny.

"Yeah, as soon as I ran to a safe location away from you guys I called my contact and changed the rendezvous location, minus one Desert Eagle 44 Magnum but still very happy not to get locked up with a weapon in my possession, man, I do miss that gun!" he said as if missed a good friend.

In an exasperated sigh, Danny wondered out loud "Holy shit Sal, just what we needed, sounds like a Watergate sized scandal to me, no?"

"Damn," was all I could muster to say. My euphoria of escaping certain death began to wane as alarm bells reverberated in my head after hearing what Manuel just recounted. Was this drug dealer telling the truth or was he trying to hide some part of his operation in the U.S. I thought to myself. If true, this was corruption by Federal officials at the highest level. I was certain of one thing, after working twenty-five years in the nation's capitol, I knew the Federal Government structure was gamed. So, becoming a whistleblower against powerful Federal officials usually results in massive retaliation and a life left in ruins! My experience had solidified a belief system that there's a visible government that citizens see and hear but behind that are several shadow governing entities that actually are the ones running our country. Hence, I worried about me and Danny and our families getting pulled into a never ending quagmire. I made a mental note to speak with Danny that maybe we shouldn't mention this story to the Feds once we turn Cicatriz over to the Border Patrol.

I took a deep breath and told Manuel, "I don't know what to make of what you told us, we'll have to let it roll in our heads for a while but for now I think it's time for me and Danny to get that asshole across the border. I hope this all works out for you and your family! I wish we had gotten the crates but you saved our skin so the only thing left to say is, hope you live a long and healthy life and away from trouble!"

"Same here Manuel, take good care. We'll get this Cabrón back to America and out of your life," Danny avowed.

We all shook hands with Manuel and Jorge then Manuel smiled and responded, "Me and my primo will be fine. My posse dug out twenty crates full of mostly gold coins and have them stashed in a safe place. Once we sell the coins, me and my men plan on disappearing."

We looked at each other and sure we were thinking the same thing, we just cheated certain death now having a pleasant chat in the middle of nowhere with drug cartel killers armed with automatic weapons. We were both getting antsy and knew the time was right to depart post-haste to the American side of the border. "Manuel, we're ready to roll out of here," Danny declared.

Manuel responded as usual in a sure and authoritative manner. "OK you guys, listen, we are between Naco and Agua Prieta. You follow this dirt road for about three miles, there's a small break in the border fence where you can squeeze through and enter America without much of a Border Patrol presence."

I confirmed Manuel's instructions with a head nod and a thumbs-up. By this time Cicatriz was fully conscious and screaming bloody murder through the rag that was still in his mouth. I removed the rag and he exploded with a tirade of threats in Spanish and Spanglish so we kept his wrists flex-cuffed behind his back. This once powerful kingpin calmed down enough to gulp down a bottle of water which I held for him.

I ordered Cicatriz to stand up and tried helping him to his feet but instead he went limp and resisted. This wasn't a new experience for me, a simple pain compliance, finger come-along lock made him scream loud enough to wake the dead but he sure sprung up off the ground like a jack-in-the-box. With a pain compliance incentive to cooperate, I ordered Cicatriz, "Now Señor, walk!" I told in in a soft but firm voice.

We started walking toward the trail when one of Manuel's men yelled out, "SUV coming very fast!"

Manuel got his binoculars and focused on the vehicle which was about two miles away. "Shit, it may be trouble. Danny, Sal, get Cicatriz the hell out of here now, move!"

Manuel and his men quickly ran to their vehicles and as they were departing Manuel leaned out his window, flashed a big grin and yelled, "Hey Danny, that Cabrón is all yours, take care, Santa Claus!" With that, Manuel and his posse sped off in the direction of the vehicle that was bearing down on us, that was our cue to beat feet.

We moved fast, bounding around big and small rocks trying to avoid prickly thickets and cactus that were all over the narrow trail, all the while pushing Cicatriz's fat ass. Whenever he tried dragging his feet the ole finger lock pain compliance made him rethink his unhelpful strategy.

After about ten minutes we heard an extended gun battle with automatic weapons and a several explosions. Not knowing what had gone down between Manuel's posse and whoever was approaching, I called out to Danny, "let's pick up the pace!"

Danny replied, "Definitely, we have about a fifteen minute lead on them but his majesty is slowing us down. With that threat in mind, we sprang into a fast jog.

We continued up and down the goat trail with Cicatriz complaining every step of the way. As we got closer to the border, we observed shoes, clothing and water jugs strewn throughout the trail. Cicatriz, also realized we were getting closer to the border and became even more belligerent and started in with the threats, "Look you two, Manuel and his men are already dead. I have a lot of men operating in your country, if you two want avoid the same fate you'll free me now. You do want to keep your families safe, no?"

In unison and without even looking up we replied, "Shut up, keep walking!"

Cicatriz then tried to bribe us with outrageous amounts of money. "I offer you one million dollars each in cash if you let me loose right now," he said with a hint of desperation in his voice.

I got sick and tired of this low life, first threatening us then trying to bribe us, so I gave him a gentle tap to his ass with my foot and ordered him, "keep walking Cabrón, you have a three day pass to Disneyland."

We came upon a rocky stretch just off the trail where we encountered two skeletons half-buried under the desert sands. The two grimacing hollow skulls had round holes in the temple area as if they had been executed and left for the buzzards, not even the solace of a decent burial.

After seeing the skeletons we moved on the trail with more caution. We frequently looked down to scan tracks in the trail as well listen for sounds of human traffickers or drug smugglers who might be on the trail.

The rest of the trek was me and Danny quietly jibber jabbing. I turned toward Danny and asked, "What you think will happen to our rental truck?"

"What, you're worried about the rental truck?"

"Yeah, just thinking out loud, did you get a chance to read the rental agreement, did our insurance cover theft of the vehicle?"

In an incredulous tone Danny replied, "Are you shitting me, that's what you're worried about, that stupid truck? We nearly got skinned alive plus we lost millions in gold. What the hell made you think of that at this very moment?"

I shrugged and said, "I don't know, a thought just popped into my head that we might have to buy the rental company a new truck especially now that we're going home with empty pockets."

Danny immediately interjected, "Sal, let me put your mind at ease, yes, our pickup truck is gone but it was fully insured so we have nothing to worry about!"

"Phew!" I replied, "I thought we were in trouble there for a second.

Danny kept walking but shot me a look of disbelief.

While still walking at a good pace and scanning around Danny called out, "you think Manuel and his men survived the gun battle?"

"I sure hope so partner but in this country survival is transitory."

Danny shaking his head asked rhetorically, "Can you believe what just happened? What are the odds of a guy we gave a break to in D.C. saves our hind parts more than a year later in another country?"

Without missing a beat, I responded, "Well, the odds are about eleven million to one! That's about how much gold we let slip through our fingers. But without your Irish luck, we would have been pig food," as we both laughed and kept on pushing northward. "Danny this is no bullshit, would the ordeal we've been through make a great movie or what?"

Danny threw his head back and gave out a huge guffaw, "Sure Sal, you're right, you should pitch the script to a Hollywood studio!" as he continued to walk and laugh. Eventually we encountered stretches of scrub thickets and undergrowth that were getting more dense all around us. As the trail grew into the faintest hint of a path, the thickets tore at our pants and shirts and scratched our arms but after a period of time we cleared nature's obstacle course eventually opening to nothing but desert sands.

2 HOURS LATER

We crested a hill and there it was, finally, beautiful American soil on the other side of a barrier that looked more like a rusted out hull of a ship than a border fence. We scampered down the hill and as we got closer to the fence we quickly spotted the hole in the corroded fence that Manuel insisted was there. "Spot on Manuel!" I said out loud.

"Dude's been right every time," marveled Danny. We quickened our pace and occasionally had to prod Cicatriz, who now had a look of terror on his face. We slid through the narrow opening in the a corrugated steel fence and had to shove hard to get Cicatriz through the hole as he wailed away poetical damnations at us in Spanglish.   Me and Danny looked at each other and laughed at the tough formidable cartel kingpin who just a few hours ago was going to carve us up like a Thanksgiving turkey.

Once over the border line and back on American soil, Danny stopped and exclaimed with joy, "Let's take it all in Sal, thank God we're Americans, I'm never leaving this country again!"

"You're right brother, it's great to be home but don't be so hasty, you know the saying, 'never say never.'

Danny decided to be a good host and said to Cicatriz, "Welcome to America Señor, it's time to take you drat the nearest U.S. Customs office. I'm sure they'll be very happy to meet with you!"   Cicatriz mumbled some shit that was unintelligible as we pushed on hoping to find a road or some semblance of civilization. In any event, it wasn't too long before civilization found us. Within fifteen minutes of entering the U.S., two Border Patrol SUV's screeched to a halt in front of us. The men in green uniforms gave us a hearty welcome to America salute by gun facing us and ordering us to our knees with our hands up.

I yelled out, "Hey that's no way to say welcome back home!"

"Quiet Sal, we don't want to get shot now that we're on American soil, not after what we've been through!"

Nonetheless, me, Danny and Cicatriz were handcuffed and searched. The agents found our police ID's and asked, "you two retired cops?"

"Yep" we replied in unison.

"How about this man, a Mexican national, why is he cuffed?

"Yep, he's the head of a drug cartel and wanted by U.S. Federal agencies," I replied.

The agents looked at each other and the one said, "Well, no sweat, we'll get this all sorted out at the station."

We were transported to a Border Patrol station and put into holding cells which was a bit disheartening. As a footnote, we never found out what the Border Patrol did with Cicatriz because we never saw him again while we were incarnated at the Border Patrol station.

Approximately two hours after arriving at the station, an investigator from U.S. Customs entered our cell and conducted an interview or maybe it was a chat to find out who the hell we were and what the hell we were doing with Cicatriz. The investigator knew we were retired cops so he didn't try any investigator BS and just tried to get the facts. He confirmed to us that indeed Cicatriz was an HVT (High Value Target) and was wanted by U.S. Federal agencies. He warned us that since we illegally extradited Cicatriz into the U.S., we may be facing legal trouble.   It was at that point that I changed my mind and decided to inform the investigator of what Manuel told us about how Cicatriz was allegedly bribing U.S. officials and obtaining U.S. passports and Green Cards for individuals from the Middle East.

The investigator drew in a deep breath and said in a low voice, "boys, this interview is over, don't tell me anything else!" he exclaimed with a worried look on his face. He walked out of the cell block, locked the door behind him, then stared at us for a brief second and shook his head as if he wanted no part of this matter.

Danny looked at me and whispered, "I thought you said not to talk about the passport thing? You think revealing that info is going to help us?"

"I don't know partner but I got desperate when he told us we might be in legal jeopardy, so I threw a Hail

Mary and hoped it would help us," I said with a bit of regret at the possible repercussions.

The following morning we were visited by another guy in a suit who claimed to be an FBI agent who flashed his 'Federal Agent' credentials like a magician performing a card trick. Ordinarily we would have asked to read his ID card and not just a quick peek at his Cracker Jack box badge flashing bullshit but we were in no position to ask anything at this point. The only thing this dude wanted to know was the issue with the passports and not even a hint of Cicatriz being illegally extradited into the U.S.

We didn't know what to make of the black suit guy but both of us doubted that he was an actual law enforcement agent but rather an intelligence spook from one of the A-B-C intel agencies. One thing is for sure, the next morning the atmosphere at the Border Patrol station changed radically as if Rasputin had risen from the grave for the sixth time because loud orders were being shouted by supervisors and agents scrambling all over the station. A border patrol captain came into the prisoner holding area and informed us that Federal officials in Washington had intervened in their protocols and had assumed full jurisdiction of our matter. He further advised that U.S. Marshals were in route to take custody of us and transport us to the Washington, D.C. region. The captain said in his thirty years on the force he'd never seen this happen before. Me and Danny looked at each other and shrugged not knowing if this was good or bad news.

The following morning no less than seven U.S. Deputy Marshals arrived and took us out of the Border Patrol station and hustled us into an SUV. Then at warp speed a caravan of SUV's took us to a remote landing strip. It was apparent this was an abandoned airport, or at least that was how it was designed to appear with no visible air traffic controls in sight. Within moments we approached a corporate type jet on the tarmac waiting with engines running.

Waiting, was another boat load of agents standing guard around the jet. We were handed off to those agents and as soon as the agents fastened our seat belts (we were still cuffed), they took their seats. The lead agent spoke into his sleeve microphone and the plane took off almost vertically like a NASA rocket.

Me and Danny were seated in separate rows with an agent seated in front and one behind us. Our hands were cuffed in the front so we were able to have a meal and a bottle of water but no conversations between us or with the Marshals, all too surreal. After about a four hour flight we landed at Ronald Reagan Washington National Airport away from the commercial terminals, near a non-descript isolated hanger. We deplaned then were turned over to another bunch of suited, armed dudes who I can only assume were other Marshals. Once again we were hustled into an SUV, then a motorcade from Arlington, Virginia to the Central Cell Block in the District of Columbia where we were incarcerated in an obscure, no longer used wing of the jail.

"Damn! Back to where we started some twenty-five years ago. Except we're on the wrong side of the bars this time," Danny groused with a heavy sigh.

13

P.N.G.'D AGAIN BUT WITH PARTING GIFTS

Every new beginning comes from some other beginning's end. - Seneca the Elder

As best I can recall we were in the central cellblock for two to three days. We were in a wing that dates back to the 1870's which contained a row of only six holding cells no longer used except for me and Danny, go figure! The advantage of this setup was that we had cells to ourselves and we could communicate liberally with each other. Having said that, other than our daily interaction with correction's officers, we were completely isolated from the world. The officers brought us food and newspapers to read. We would often shoot the shit with them and they were as dumfounded as we were as to why we were being held incommunicado in the old abandoned wing.

Our time in the cellblock consisted of a workout regime several times a day of running in place, to pushup and sit-up competitions with each other to joking and finally to total depression. We lingered in those cells without a word from anyone, not even our family but it was the not knowing what was going on that was driving us to despondency. It was on our last day that Danny lamented out loud for the twenty-fifth time, "I can't believe after a twenty-five year police career I wind up in jail in my own jurisdiction!"

Always trying to remain positive, I responded to Danny's wailing, "Let's look on the positive side, a few days ago we were pig food, we're alive and maybe the Feds will take into consideration that we extradited a Narco-terrorist."

Of course Danny was out of sorts and I knew would roar back at me, "Shut up Sal, not another word! What about our family? What about our kids? I mean . ." but before he finished his sentence two corrections officers approached our cell with four men in suits following behind them.

The corrections officer unlocked our cell door allowing the four guys in suits to enter our cell. One of the corrections officer called out, "Rossi, Mahoney the two of you are being transported to another location. Effective immediately you are in the custody of these four gentlemen."

One of the black suited guys announced, "Men, we are deputies with the U.S. Marshal's Service." They all simultaneously flashed their credentials giving us enough time to verify who they were. "Put your hands against the wall and spread your legs we have to check you guys for any weapons or contraband.

We both complied but after being locked down like we were the second coming of Lee Oswald, I was getting more pissed by the second and ready to pop a cork but I kept my cool. The Deputies searched us then handcuffed us behind our backs. We were escorted to the Sally Port where two Suburban's with blacked out tinted windows were waiting. We were placed in the rear bench seat that had a bullet proof barrier dividing us from the other compartments. As soon as we were out of the underground garage, I inquired, "Where we going?" No response from the Marshals who remained silent.

I asked a second time and the agent snapped, "Listen up, you're being transported to another Federal facility. You will be handed off to personnel at that location. Do not ask us who, what, where, when or how because we don't know that much of this matter. Enjoy the ride, it may the last time you guys see the outdoors for a while, understood?"

We answered in unison, "Yes sir," as we glanced at each other with worried looks.

We sat quietly taking in the sights, the Washington Monument, the Capitol and the White House. Danny quipped with a sigh, "Still not the best circumstances but it feels good being back in America, I'm never leaving it again!" The two Suburban's pulled into the driveway of a tall building and were stopped by an armed, uniformed security guard standing by the entry of an underground garage. The Suburban driver rolled down his window, flashed his ID and the security guard waved us through without one word ever exchanged. We drove down a ramp into a huge underground parking lot and pulled into an isolated section near an elevator. The deputies removed us from the vehicle and ordered us to turn around. To our surprise they took the handcuffs off at which point the lead agent announced, "Look gentlemen, we follow orders like you guys did when you were cops here in D.C., so no hard feelings OK. You guys get on that elevator, just press the only button which is UP. The elevator will take you straight to your floor! Agents will be waiting for you and escort you to your destination. Good luck to you both!" The agents extended their hands and we shook hands with all of them.

We walked to the elevator with caution as this situation became even more surreal. We did as instructed, got in the elevator pressed the only button and I muttered out loud, "Strange shit, ay Danny?"

"Yeah, I don't get this whole thing, one minute we're in jail in handcuffs, now we're on an elevator alone, how's this movie going to end?" I estimate we travelled about eight floors, once the elevator doors opened, four agents in dark suits were waiting. The lead agent quickly said, "Mr. Rossi, Mr. Mahoney please follow me."

"Twilight Zone," I whispered under my breath. We followed the agents down a long hallway which had oil paintings on the walls that looked like masterpieces. This place looked more like a museum than a Federal office building. We continued following the one agent while the other three agents walked behind us and just wondered what the hell these people think we might do, make a run for it?

We came to a door that was about twelve feet tall made out of solid oak. The lead agent opened the door and grandeur of the office struck us immediately. The office had an incredibly high ceiling adorned with religious and Masonic images, the walls were lined with glossy Brazilian wood paneling and expansive bookshelves filled with ornate, leather-bound books.

When we finally stopped looking around we realized there was a gray haired man in a pin striped suit, sitting behind a huge, hand carved mahogany desk, smoking a cigarette with his back to the door. Two Victorian style chairs were facing his desk.

Without turning around to face us, the man said, "Mr. Rossi, Mr. Mahoney, welcome, please have a seat."

The lead agent pointed to the two chairs and ordered, "have a seat!"

The man behind the desk swiveled his chair around facing us. With a benevolent glare directed at us he said, "Agents, thank you, that will be all for now. I'll call for you after our business is finished."

The lead agent responded, "Yes Sir," as he waved his hand to his three fellow agents, then exited the room and closed the door behind them without saying another word.

"Hello gentlemen, my name is not so important but feel free to call me DeMolay. I realize this is all a lot to take in but this is how we handle these types of sensitive matters. First and foremost, I have to advise you that this meeting is being visually and audio recorded. Do you understand that?"

We nodded our heads but DeMolay immediately spoke up, "Negative, gentlemen I need a verbal reply from each one of you. Mr. Rossi do you understand? "

I responded, "Yes sir.""

"Mr. Mahoney?"

"Yes sir I understand we are being recorded and video-taped!"

"Excellent, next question, are you willing to speak to me without legal representation present?"

I replied, "Well, what is all this? What do you want from us?"

Danny elbowed me with a serious look on his face said, "let's play along!"

"Yes sir, we're willing hear what you have to say without an attorney present," I politely replied.

DeMolay took a deep drag on his cigarette. "Good choice that will speed up our business greatly! Gentlemen, I am a Senior Executive Service Level one, that's about high as you can get in our government. I'm often called on by powerful people in and out of our government to fix problems here at home or overseas and keep them out of the news media for one reason or another."

We didn't know what this DeMolay guy was getting to so we both said that we understood he had the highest civilian rank in the Federal Government.

DeMolay continued, "Right out of the chute I gotta tell you boys, you are in a world of shit. For starters, your antics have put our government in one helluva bind!

You've entered the U.S. illegally through a non-point of entry and extradited a Mexican citizen into the U.S. without extradition documents. So technically speaking even though this individual is also wanted by the Mexican Federales, the Government is pissed and accusing the United States in general, and you two specifically, of kidnapping one of their citizens!"

I couldn't believe what I was hearing and snapped at DeMolay, "So you're going to send that asshole back to México?"

"Certainly not, that S.O.B. is going to fill in the blanks for our Intel agencies about terrorist cells he's met with in the Middle East and names of terrorists he's helped cross into the U.S. From México and as they say, possession is nine tenths of the law. Mr. Francisco "Cicatriz" Gutierrez is staying right here in the U.S."

So that's the asshole's real name I thought to myself! I looked at Danny and the gentle giant was sitting with his hands clasped like a defendant in court waiting to hear the sentence.

DeMolay continued, "So, that's where I come in. I need to make this mess go away." DeMolay paused and took a deep drag from his cigarette.

I took his pause as a sign that maybe there was a ray of hope for our predicament so I blurted out, "OK great, what about us? Do we get some credit for turning him over to the Feds?"

"Well Mr. Rossi it's like this, you put our government in a difficult situation with the Mexican Government and Latin America in general. If this incident leaks out there'll be protests throughout the Americas and beyond about how America the superpower can violate other country's sovereignty whenever they want, you follow?"

We both nodded our heads in agreement and understanding.

"The other problem that needs fixing is that several Federal agencies have tracked the gold ore and gems you extracted in Afghanistan and shipped to the U.S. I can't even begin to tell you the laws you've violated plus the fines and back taxes you two are liable for."

"Holy shit, they're going to bankrupt us first then send us to prison," Danny fretted under his breath.

I nodded at Danny, I was already irritated at how we'd been treated since entering the U.S. but now listening to this additional crap, my self-control was fraying. I was ready to blow a gasket so in less than an articulate manner, I boomed out, "So what the hell do you want from us? What's this cloak and dagger shit all about?"

DeMolay remained cool and calm, not even the slightest hint of concern at my outburst as he continued, "All good questions Mr. Rossi but your reality is that right this very minute you are facing a sizeable list of felony charges with several Federal agencies chomping at the bit to get their hands on you two for criminal prosecution. However, certain powerful people have intervened and have called on me to fix this shit show and make it go away. Let me lay a few facts on you. You are facing a minimum 10 years in a Federal penitentiary just for your antics in México, not to mention the gold and precious gems you mined in Afghanistan without that country's permission and not reporting them on your tax returns!"

I quickly replied, "wait a damn minute . ."

Danny abruptly interrupted me and said, "Sal, we're in deep shit, let's just let this play out and see what happens!" But before I could answer Danny, DeMolay continued, "The fact is you two owe about $50,000 in back taxes from your caper in Afghanistan along with a $50,000 dollar fine each for failing to report your mining income. Lastly, our government has been in talks with Mexican officials and they have agreed to terms to make the violations of their sovereignty disappear. To demonstrate our remorse of this unfortunate incident, our government has agreed to upgrade their Federal police training center with a couple of state-of-the-art indoor ranges and Firearms Training Simulator along with an assortment of weapons and a ton of ammunition. Of course this is going to cost money, to the tune of about ten million dollars."

The ambiguity of what we were hearing was too much even for the mild tempered Danny who threw his arms up in the air, "Are you shitting us, so what the hell you telling us, that we owe the government more than ten million dollars? Where the hell would we get that much, you do know that we did not recover the gold! So what is it, you talking about the Feds garnishing our pension?"

Again DeMolay remained calm, took a long drag of his cigarette and swiveled his chair away from us without a hint of fear that we would jump out of our seats and yoke him out, this dude was one cool cat!

DeMolay, still with his back to us, remarked, "I can only assume you don't know how much the U.S. Government has wanted to get their hands on Mr. Francisco "Cicatriz" Gutierrez." He swiveled his chair back around to face us, took one last drag of his cigarette and extinguished it on the ashtray. "Boys our government has a sort of bounty savings account that contains funds to pay out rewards for assistance in capturing the most wanted high value individuals. In this account sits thirty million dollars that we are lawfully required to pay off, if and when an American or foreigner leads to the capture of Mr. Mr. Francisco "Cicatriz" Gutierrez."

Without revealing a hint of excitement, I took an internal sigh of relief, this was a cheerful-earful that maybe we were not in for a lengthy incarceration.

DeMolay continued, "So even though Mr. Francisco "Cicatriz" Gutierrez was captured and extradited to the U.S. in a less than legal manner, by statutory law, someone has to get that thirty million dollar bounty."

Like synchronized swimmers, me and Danny turned and looked at each other at the exact same time. I let that information roll around my head for a hot second, and responded with skepticism, "What the hell are you saying, that we're entitled to that reward?" I asked with a bit more control.

DeMolay stared at us for about ten uncomfortable seconds and replied, "It's a conundrum on so many levels men but in actuality, the bottom line is, yes, you two malcontents are entitled to that money."

I jumped out my chair, grabbed Danny's shoulders and yelled, "I knew this was going to work out, I knew it!" The big Irishman just sat there with a numb expression of relief that things were finally breaking our way!

"Mr. Rossi, sit your ass down, there's more!"

Danny uttered, "Oh shit, here it comes!" I sat back down slowly trying to prepare for what 'there's more' meant!

"Having said all that, let's discuss what exactly you're entitled to." DeMolay picked up a sheet of paper from a stack on his desk and started elaborating. "The I.R.S. needs to collect their portion of the 30 million dollar reward, which comes to 5.4 million dollars. Each of you owe $13,500 dollars in back taxes and a $50,000 dollar penalty for failing to report income!   Lastly, we need 10 million dollars for the Mexican police training facility enhancement package."

"OK, OK, now what?" I asked with skepticism.

DeMolay continued, "So, of that 30 million dollar bounty the government will collect a little over 15 million dollars to makes things right. This leaves about $14,473,000 dollars for you two to split which is approximately $7,236,500 each, give or take a few pesos!" DeMolay said with the first hint of a grin forming around the edge of his lips.

Saying nothing else, DeMolay who had already knocked out three cigs now removed a fourth from a pack on his desk, lit it, took a few deep carcinogenic drags and nonchalantly asked, "Is everything I just enumerated acceptable to you both, I need a verbal response, please."

Danny answered first, "Yes sir, very acceptable."

I was still skeptical that there was more to come so I followed Danny's affirmation with just a, "Yes sir."

"Excellent, let's continue because there's one thing more."

"Here it comes," Danny said staring straight ahead.

DeMolay picked up a document from his desk and said, "Before your status of incarceration can change to something else, you both must sign a two page Non-Disclosure and Conditional Agreement."

"Do we get to read these forms before signing?" I asked.

DeMolay responded immediately, "In fact, yes, I need you both to carefully read the first page only. Don't bother with the second page, it's all shadow government legalese that you won't understand and will consume more of my time, which I have precious little of. So you'll have to trust me on this one Señor Rossi."

"Do we get a copy of what we're signing?" I asked again.

DeMolay seemed annoyed with my question and tersely replied, "No, Mr. Rossi, it's a take it or leave it proposition and believe me, it's the most incredibly generous arrangement I've ever been part of! So here, read it, fully grasp the stipulations you are agreeing to!" He pushed the documents on his desk toward us.

I stared at the multi-page legal document and even with our law enforcement background I couldn't make heads or tails of the mumbo jumbo legalese. I thought to myself that signing this document probably had future repercussions but I was ready to sign anything just to get the hell out of this building!

I began reading page one.

Section I:

By the rules governing petitions for presidential clemency, this document intending to be legally bound, in consideration of the awards listed in Section II, I hereby accept the obligations contained in section III of this Agreement.

Holy shit, a presidential pardon, what the hell are we involved in, I thought to myself but I continued reading.

Section II

1. *Mr. Salvatore Rossi and Mr. Daniel Mahoney purchasing a winning Florida lottery ticket together agree to split Fourteen million, four-hundred seventy-three thousand dollars after tax proceeds.*

2. *Mr. Salvatore Rossi is officially listed as "Persona Non Grata" in an agreement with the governments of Afghanistan and Mexico. Mr. Salvatore Rossi will be subject to arrest and*

prosecution should he attempt or enter the enumerated countries.

Section III

1. *Mr. Salvatore Rossi is subject to subpoena as a material witnesses in any grand jury or trial proceedings or be recalled to travel to CONUS or OCONUS in any future investigations involving any and all matters relating to Mr. Francisco "Cicatriz." Gutierrez. This section remains in full effect for five years from the date of this document.*

2. *Prosecution of Mr. Salvatore Rossi for violations of Immigration and tax evasion as enumerated in United States Code of laws is held in abeyance pending the completion of all matters relating to Mr. Francisco "Cicatriz" Gutierrez or five years from the date of this document or whichever comes first.*

I have been advised and fully agree that any breach of this agreement may result in prosecution of 18 U.S. Code Title 18—Crimes and Criminal Procedures and laws.

I have read this agreement carefully and my questions, if any, have been answered.

Danny lifted his eyes from the document and looked at DeMolay then asked, "What's this about us having a winning lottery ticket?"

"Not a big deal in the scheme of things Mr. Mahoney, the fact is that we have agreements with a few

States that lend a hand in covert circumstances such as this. In your case we struck a deal with the State of Florida whereby they assist the Federal Government in making the funds associated with this case legit and in return they're promised a piece of a pending Federal contract, so they make out at the end!"

Danny shook his head in disbelief and replied, "Ah . . mind-boggling but guess I can wrap my head around it."

"Yeah, I guess I get it too," I replied, "Now can you clarify what stipulation number three obligates us to?"

"Gentlemen, the investigation into Francisco "Cicatriz" Gutierrez and his associates appears to have far reaching implications that possibly reaches the highest level of our government. There's no telling what the outcome will be or the possible inter agency wars that may result.

Me and Danny glanced at each other probably thinking the same thing, damn we're not going to make a clean break from this tar baby!

DeMolay continued, "If we need you to testify or travel to a foreign country then you are obligated to do so, it's just that simple. You two are on the hook until the investigation has concluded."

I leaned over to Danny and asked him, "What you think partner?"

Danny didn't answer me instead he asked, DeMolay, "So you're telling us that you have the power to let us just walk out of here free men and someday we'll get sixteen million dollars?"

"You sign this agreement here and now, I can assure you the money will appear in your bank accounts in less than one minute."

In a hushed voice Danny leaned toward me and said, "lets sign these shitty papers and get the hell out of here before we get sent back to the central cell block!"

"Agreed brother!" I replied.

"How do we verify the money has been wired to our bank?" I inquired.

De Molay opened his desk drawer and pulled out two cell phones. These are encrypted phones, we took the liberty of programming the number for each of your financial institutions. But first things first, sign the agreement!" We looked at each other, nodded and signed the documents.

DeMolay responded with a booming voice "excellent!" He removed a cellphone from his suit breast pocket, pressed a button and within a few seconds was speaking to someone. "Wire the funds now, account number T41846." He disconnected the line and told us to standby. After about a minute of staring at each other he handed us each a cell phone and instructed us to call our bank.

We quickly saw our bank telephone number pre-programmed in the cellphones so we proceeded as directed to call our bank.. Very quickly this whole encounter became even more surreal as we were stunned that our checking accounts had a balance of seven million plus dollars.

"Money there?" DeMolay inquired with a smile.

In unison we respond in disbelief, "Yes!"

DeMolay then handed us our tri-fold wallets containing our police ID's and said, "There's a few dollars in there for incidentals you may need to get back home."

We just wanted to get the hell out of there so we put the wallets away quickly without looking at the contents. With that done, DeMolay announced, "Gentlemen, our business has concluded."

"Now what?" I asked with a ton of trepidation.

Without responding to my question he pressed a button under his desk and the same four men in suits quickly entered his office.

"My business with these men has concluded, we're going with plan A so please escort these men to their destination, understand?"

The lead agent responded by repeating, "Plan A, will do sir."

What the hell was plan A, I contemplated.

The lead agent approached us and ordered, "Gentlemen, let's go!"

We got up and Danny asked the agents, "Hey guys, can you handcuff us in the front? That cuffing behind my back is killing my shoulders!"

All the agents chuckled and the lead agent matter-of-factly replied, "No handcuffs this time men, follow me." We followed the lead agent out of the office while the three other agents trailed behind us giving us an uneasy feeling that maybe there were other law enforcement personnel waiting to take us into custody. We just had no idea what was happening so we went along with the movie script.

We were almost in the hallway when DeMolay called out to us, "Hey! One last thing before you two leave!" The agents took the cue and halted the escort. DeMolay took a deep drag on his cigarette and said, "I've seen a lot of incredible shit in my time but you two," he paused, "you've been PNG'd out of two countries in less than two years and . . "

I turned to Danny and whispered, "There's that damn PNG word again!"

DeMolay continued, "I'm convinced you two have shit for brains and God only knows how the hell you survived attacks from the Taliban and Mexican Cartels. But, but one thing I'm also absolutely convinced of, you men have balls of steel! For your own good and for the good of our nation, forget anymore crazy shit ideas, enjoy your money and your freedom! Now get outta here!" DeMolay, who was sporting a huge smile on his face, saluted us and finished by saying, "Good luck to both of you!"

We saluted him back and kept on walking with the agents.

The agents led us through several corridors then to an elevator that went straight down with no stops, leading to a long tunnel. We traversed the length of the tunnel and came to a huge metal double door. The lead agent opened the door and said, "Good luck to you both!" We walked out and heard the door slam shut behind us. There we were, the intersection of 17th Street and E Street.

Danny looked dazed and said, "Man is this a trick, are we dreaming, what the hell just happened?"

"Danny, do you recognize this building because I sure shit don't?"

"No idea, why?" he shot back.

"I mean we're blocks away from the Whitehouse for goodness sake! Follow me, this building has got to have an agency designation!" We walked to the front of the building and not only did it not have a name on it but there were armed guards in the lobby. "Sheeeet, this must be a black site for one of the A-B-C intel agencies," I muttered out loud as the guards stared at us through the glass doors.

"C'mon Sal, let's get the hell out of here!"

I wanted to know more of who the hell we were dealing with because we had absolutely no proof of what we signed or even what agency DeMolay belonged to. But at the end of the day, the bottom line was, what the hell, we were free, with a ton of money in the bank, so all I could say to Danny was, "Right on, let's go."

I felt a wave of exultation and a concrete weight lifted from my soul so I let out a loud shout, "it's real Danny, we're free!" I ran up and down the street simply because I could and not locked up in a dingy cell block. The pedestrians around us kept going about their business but occasionally glanced a concerned look at us certainly convinced that I was a homeless crazy person. Hell, I didn't care, in just a week's time we were nearly carved up into pieces and fed to a herd of pigs, we'd been incarcerated and put in isolation and now freedom plus a few million dollars in the bank, just mind-boggling!

"Hey, before we head home let's get a steak dinner and beer," I blurted out.

Danny thought about it for a few seconds then replied, "With what money?"

I didn't even think about having money so I removed my wallet from my pocket, I looked inside and counted ten one-hundred dollar bills. "Right on DeMolay!" Danny looked in his wallet and he also had one thousand dollars in cash.

We found an upscale restaurant, satiated our hunger and then it was time to get our asses home to our families. We quickly hailed a couple of taxis, gave each other a double high-five while laughing heartily at our unreal experience then we went our separate ways back to our homes.

14

ONE LAST TIME

I'm never less at leisure than when at leisure. – Scipio

"Twelve months later…"

As you can imagine a lot happened since our release from Federal incarceration. Most importantly, we all breathed a sigh of relief that we had not been contacted by any Federal agency regarding the Cicatriz matter. It's fair to say that for the first time since my retirement from the PD, I've been able to enjoy the freedom and lower- intensity of everyday life. Jean and I have gotten a lot closer emotionally and we're simply content.

Our son's grueling application process to the U.S. Military Academy was successful. We were extremely proud that our son, West Point Cadet Victor D. Rossi, who earned his appointment from his congressman and is now proudly representing the State of Maryland at the Academy.

So after about a month of sleep and rest, Jean and I packed up our new Range Rover SUV and headed north on the six hour drive to West Point, New York. We had a great visit with Victor and I felt very much at ease not having to wear a polo shirt or jacket to hide a holstered handgun.

Sometime thereafter, we sold our home in Maryland and bought a beachfront house in Florida. Yeah, hot and humid nine months of the year but at least I got the Maryland tax collectors out of my pockets.

Besides buying the home in Florida, we took a two week wonders of Britain and Ireland vacation which Jean had been dreaming of for decades. We also made sure to square away any money issues for close family members. The remaining funds from our bounty was invested in a ten year U.S. Treasury bond that was paying five percent, and yielded a sizeable six figure yearly income or about seven times my police pension. We definitely had enough to enjoy a very comfortable life.

However, one day when Jean was out shopping, I was sitting in my den and decided to open my 'gray file' which I hadn't seen in more than two years. The file is actually a withered manila file folder, bulging with newspaper and magazine clippings of treasure stories and American POW's from S.E. Asia stories that had piqued my interest during the past three-plus decades since joining the Corp in 1970. The inside of the folder is completely covered with handwritten personal thoughts and assumptions as to the veracity of each story along with names of contacts, phone numbers and addresses. As if it was predestined, the clippings of my notes on the bearer bonds story during the fall of South Vietnam fell out of the folder and unto my lap. Suddenly, the pang of unfinished business screamed in my head, why the hell not!

'Thirty days later…'

Jean and I were northbound on I-95 in route to Middleburg, Virginia to visit the big Irishman and his wife Becky. The drive itself would have ordinarily taken about twelve hours but both of us being history buffs and having a great interest in old cemeteries along with off the beaten path roadside attractions, the trip took us three-plus days. The first stop on the way north was historic Jekyll Island Georgia where, at the turn of the century, six ultra-wealthy men met at Jekyll Island and organized what eventually became the Federal Reserve banking system. We then stopped at the Bonaventure Cemetery also in Georgia, Ft Bragg Museum in North Carolina, the Garrett farm roadside marker in Port Royal, Virginia that identifies the barn where John Wilkes Booth was tracked down and killed and finally Colonial Williamsburg where we spent the better part of a full day.

Eventually we made it to the Middleburg Virginia and located Danny's home. As we approached the driveway we had that wow moment, the shit was definitely impressive. Clearly Danny was living the life of a Virginia country squire. His French-designed country manor was nestled in twenty private acres of rolling hills and woodlands filled with majestic oaks, the place was right out of a magazine for the rich and famous.

We were greeted at the door by Becky who led us in and to the back of the house where Danny, his two daughters, and their friends were rollicking, having a good time. We sat around the expansive patio, gazing into the dazzling Olympic size pool while having sandwiches and ice-cold, Mexican cervezas and lemonade. Jean and Becky were involved in non-stop chatter catching up on family stuff. I motioned for Danny to walk with me out of earshot of the gals.

Becky noticed the two men walking away and with a worried look on her face, "Jean, is it even remotely possible that Sal is trying to get Danny involved in another cockamamie scheme?"

At first it seemed like such a silly question but after thinking about it for a second, Jean's eyes opened widely as disbelief crossed her face which quickly turned into a scowl as she snapped, "No way Becky, they're not going anywhere!"

Now out of earshot of the two women I probed Danny's state of mind. We walked and I listened to how he had invested his portion of the bounty, how he had pre-paid his daughter's college tuition and how all the money stressors had dissipated. I intentionally kept the conversation lighthearted and away from serious shit for a period of time.

Danny's body language and demeanor now indicated he was totally relaxed so it was time to steer the conversation to the topic at hand, "Hey, you know I'm thinking of taking a trip to Vietnam."

Danny replied, "No kidding, I just read a story that Vietnam has become a hot spot for tourism."

"Yeah, the world has discovered another place to vacation and spoil into another tourist trap," I said with rancor.

"Just you and Jean?" Danny asked.

"Well, not really . . "

"Oh?" Danny quickly inquired.

"Look, just hear me out, I know we've been through a helluva an ordeal but don't say no. Let me tell you about this story that's been in my gray file for twenty seven years."

"You're joking Sal, right? Stop right now, I'm a freakin millionaire, I don't need anything else and most of all, I ain't leaving America anytime soon!"

"No, no, there's no danger in this thing it's just a long flight, a day or two walking around, pick up a brief case with documents and return home, absolutely no drama, it's actually like a little vacation."

Danny interrupted me and snapped out his answer, "You do know that No, is a complete sentence, no!"

I let out a laugh, "you're not going to believe this one, just four little big words, ONE HUNDRED MILLION DOLLARS!"

"Sal, I don't need any more money and I'm not going anywhere!"

"Well, I'll tell you how simple this could be and think about how much better your life will be with fifty million dollars!"

"You're wasting your time but if can you tell it to me in less than five minutes, then fine cause I want to get back to the pool!"

"You betcha, listen to this. "Look, in late 1974, the Pentagon secretly funneled one-hundred million dollars in treasury bearer bonds to the South Vietnamese Government in order for them to buy ammunition and weapons on the open market. This allowed the President to deny that we were still aiding the South Vietnamese which had been prohibited by the U.S. Congress. The South Vietnamese were supposed to transfer the bonds to their European Bank accounts then purchase enough armaments to keep their military afloat, however the commies overran South Vietnamese forces in lightning speed and the south never got the chance to use the bonds. With the communist forces closing in on Saigon, it's believed that the Deputy Premier for Economic Development took the bonds and buried them in a cave near Hue City. He was allegedly the only individual privy to that information.

Danny said nothing as we walked and nodded every now and then.

I continued, "When it became evident the collapse of the south was inevitable, a covert plan was hatched by the White House administration wherein a small group of American Green Berets were to covertly deploy into Vietnam and recover the bearer bonds."

"Well, did the SPEC OP guys make it to Vietnam?"

"Well, yeah but due to the political climate in our country with everyone being fed up with the war, the

Pentagon decided to keep the risks to a minimum and actually tasked only two Army Green Berets to the dangerous and dubious mission. The dudes made it to Saigon and used their contacts in the Vietnamese government to confirm that the Economic Development minister was the one in possession of the bonds. The soldiers found that minister in Saigon, who apparently was an honorable man so he informed the soldiers that he buried a steel camera case containing the bonds in a cave in Hue City. The green beanies travelled to Hue but were met by some very bad ass North Vietnamese regulars who nearly captured both of them. The men were able to exfiltrate to Thailand but they did so empty-handed."

"And, of course, I suppose you know what cave the bonds are located in, right?"

Laughing, I replied "You bet I know where the bonds are located, they're in a very specific cave in Thua Thien, Hue Province."

"How the hell did you get this information and how the hell can you be certain that people in the know didn't go back and recover the bonds a bazillion years ago?"

"All good questions but the sequence of events in this yarn are even stranger than the Hidalgo Brothers story."

"Hell no, don't ever mention that name again, please!"

"Anyway, you know I served in the Marines from 70 – 76. After I got out I applied for the DC Police job but didn't hear anything back so I took a job that paid some pretty good cheese working as an anti-terrorism security guard on a ten thousand acre agricultural farm in Rhodesia. I was on that gig in 1977 for eight months but get this, during that time I became good drinking buddies with none other than 'Jess' one of the Green Berets on that bond recovery mission."

"Holy shit man, you're always in the right place at the right time!"

I chuckled and replied that Jean thinks I'm always in the wrong place at the wrong time!

I continued, "I guess a lot of these Spec OPS guys got used to being in combat and this dude was now working as a commander with the Rhodesian Special Forces. Well, to say this dude drank too much was an understatement. Anyway, not many Americans were working in Rhodesia so me and Jess would hang out together with a few other yanks. One night, or in reality morning, probably 0200 hours, Jess was totally wasted and came by my hooch for a nightcap. I drank one beer while Jess consumed the other five in my only six pack. So out of nowhere he recounted the entire treasury bond story from beginning to end. He told me the name of the Economic Development minister, where he supposedly buried the bonds and also informed me that his Green Beret partner on that mission had recently died of cancer, possibly due to the many years of exposure to the Agent Orange defoliation chemical."

"Jess told you about the bonds so how the hell do we know that he didn't tell others?" Danny asked showing definite interest in the story.

"Yeah, OK, what I'm about to tell you, I think, really closes the loop on most of the story. In 1979, I read a story in the Post newspaper that identified a few former South Vietnamese cabinet members who died in North Vietnamese re-education camps. The Economic Development Minister's name was on that list. Lastly, in 1984, I received correspondence from a group of Americans who had served in Rhodesia and created an informal group. The letter informed me that "Jess" had been killed in action in Angola while leading South African Defense forces. I stopped and looked directly at Danny and said, "so basically the three individuals who knew the location of the bonds are deceased, that is, except for me."

Trying to digest all the information all at once, Danny said in a pensive tone, "Damn, that's a fantastic story, we should have gone to Vietnam instead of Afghanistan!"

"Maybe so but we can still fly over there, take a quick looksee without any repercussions."

"Do you know the resulting shit storm in our house if I tell Beck that I'm leaving again on another hunt for treasure?"

"Man, you don't have to tell Becky all the details about our trip! You wouldn't be lugging around your metal detector or anything tactical! So all Beck needs to know is that you're accompanying me to Vietnam for a tour of some of the battlefield locations where I was stationed during the war."

Rubbing his chin Danny just let out an, "Aha!"

"Look, the bonds should be easy to locate since they were buried within a waterproof, aluminum camera case. My small hand held metal detector should be able to locate it quick shit! One last but very important note, these bonds belong to whoever holds them! You got that? The U.S. Government cannot claim any of it is theirs!"

"No, you sure about that?"

"Yep, says so right on the Treasury Notes, 'obligated to pay the holder'. If we recover them we bring them back to the U.S., cash them at a Federal Reserve Bank in D.C., then pay the Federal taxes on the cash out value! Another thing, this little trip won't cost you a penny because I'll buy the tickets, hotel rooms and pay all expenses, all you have to do is help me dig the case out of the cave and collect your share."

"Sal, have you even given thought that maybe our passports are somehow flagged if we attempt to the leave the U.S?"

"Brother, I had the same thought so about four months ago I took Jean on a vacation to London she's been wanting for a long time. We flew first class all the way no problems with our TSA, nor British Customs nor when we re-entered the U.S.! Our passports are clean and good-to-go! Now, the rest of the who, what, where, when and how, I'll tell you during the 26-hour flight to Ho Chi Minh City."

"Like always you've got everything covered."

"Danny, one-hundred million dollars! Let that roll around in your head for a hot second!"

"Sal, the only hot thing I'm thinking about is the hot weather and the only place I'm going is back into the pool."

I was convinced that Danny had dollar signs in his head and was hooked so I pulled out of my pocket the lucky 1907, Saint-Gaudens double eagle, gold coin.

"Put that damn shitty coin away Sal!"

I flipped the coin up in the air and yelled, "call it!" The coin struck the cement path and spun around several times.

"Three months later…"

As the Boeing 777 departs the runway at Dulles International Airport the passenger in business class, seat 2A is heard saying, "How many days did you say we have the hotel rooms reserved for? Hey, did we need a Yellow Fever Immunizations to get into the country? Where are the street maps?"

The passenger in seat 2B puts on his noise-canceling headphones, pushes the recline button on his business class, plush leather seat, kicks back with a big smile on his face, thinking about his cut of the one hundred million dollars!

Yeah, he called tails, it wasn't!

ABOUT THE AUTHOR

Paul Charuka, is a pseudonym for the author who is a retired police official that served for 25 years with four different law enforcement agencies in the Washington, D.C. region. During the past forty-five years Mr. Charuka has attained a Master's Degree from the University of Hard Knocks with a major in getting out of shit with his hind parts intact.

Paul has dabbled in various forms of martial arts, is a fluent Spanish speaker with a working knowledge of Portuguese and a 1970's U.S. Army veteran.

After hanging up his badge, gun and uniform, Paul who self-describes as a restless soul and adventurer has worked as a gun for hire as well as a trainer-advisor in far flung places in the Middle East, S.W. Asia, Africa and Latin America.

Mr. Charuka is now fully retired and under the watchful eye and supervision of his wife of forty years and resides somewhere in the Mid-Atlantic region

Connect with the author at: pcharuka@tutanota.com